A Woman Like Annie
Inglath Cooper

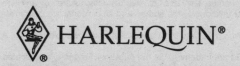

HARLEQUIN®

TORONTO • NEW YORK • LONDON
AMSTERDAM • PARIS • SYDNEY • HAMBURG
STOCKHOLM • ATHENS • TOKYO • MILAN • MADRID
PRAGUE • WARSAW • BUDAPEST • AUCKLAND

ISBN 0-373-71174-3

A WOMAN LIKE ANNIE

Copyright © 2003 by Inglath Cooper.

This edition published by arrangement with Harlequin Books S.A.

® and TM are trademarks of the publisher. Trademarks indicated with ® are registered in the United States Patent and Trademark Office, the Canadian Trade Marks Office and in other countries.

Visit us at www.eHarlequin.com

Printed in U.S.A.

A picture of Annie formed in Jack's head

As she'd looked that afternoon on the drive back, smiling, a little flushed from the craziness of the day.

He could not remember the last time he'd enjoyed a woman's company as much as he'd enjoyed Annie's today. There was something about being with her that felt natural and easy. It seemed as if they had known one another for years.

But then, everything about his attraction to Annie was different.

The admission tripped him a little, and he felt the unbalancing of the convictions he'd held on to for so long. He wondered if he had met the woman who could make him believe once and for all that real love was not a fairy tale.

Dear Reader,

I've loved books for as long as I can remember, might actually have read every title in my elementary school library. I was one of those kids who never went anywhere without one in my hand or tucked inside my bag.

I now have three precious daughters who love them, too. One of them promises to be just like me. She's a toddler, and she likes all books. Sits and looks at the pages, even when there are no pictures, just words. She's fascinated and comforted by them. That pretty much sums up how I feel about stories that let me, the reader, step into other lives for a while, meet someone I think about long after I've finished the book.

If I can do that for someone else, I will consider that my greatest accomplishment as a writer.

I love to hear from readers. Please visit my Web site at www.inglathcooper.com. Or write to me at P.O. Box 973, Rocky Mount, VA 24151.

All best,

Inglath

For Kavvi, Tatti and Nadia...sweet, sweet daughters.
My life's blessing.

And for Monica Caltabiano. Truest friend.

Books by Inglath Cooper

HARLEQUIN SUPERROMANCE
728—THE LAST GOOD MAN

Don't miss any of our special offers. Write to us at the
following address for information on our newest releases.

Harlequin Reader Service
U.S.: 3010 Walden Ave., P.O. Box 1325, Buffalo, NY 14269
Canadian: P.O. Box 609, Fort Erie, Ont. L2A 5X3

CHAPTER ONE

MAYOR ANNIE MCCABE WAS LATE.

Her meeting with Jack Corbin was not the kind of meeting a person was late for. It had taken three weeks of unreturned phone calls to get it. And in less than thirty minutes, she would be sitting across a table from the one man who had the power to prevent the town of Macon's Point from drying up and blowing right off the Virginia state map.

The population sign standing guard at the Langor County line read 3032. Anyone passing through would likely label the town nothing special. True, there was no hubbub of cultural activity at its center, no opera or art museum. Only a farmer's market and a once-monthly Friday night bluegrass jamboree. But Macon's Point had become home to Annie in the past three years.

And to her that meant something.

In the year since her divorce, Annie had found peace in this town, a certainty that she would be perfectly content to spend the rest of her life here. It was that kind of place.

The only problem?

If Jack Corbin auctioned off Corbin Manufacturing,

half the town would have to move elsewhere. Somehow, tonight, she had to find the words to make him look for another solution to the company's problems.

Meanwhile, her hair was still wet, and her blouse was missing its middle button.

"Mama?"

"What, honey?" Annie wrestled a comb through her tangled hair, glancing up with a distracted smile at her six-year-old son's reflection in the bathroom mirror. Sometimes it shocked her how much he looked like J.D. His hair was a shade of blond women tried to emulate in the priciest salons. His blue eyes had lashes thick enough to generate the same kind of envy. The one concession to cuteness over outright beauty was the dimple in each cheek.

In the father, those dimples had once made her knees go weak. In the son, she was similarly unable to frown on even the most mischievous of deeds when he turned them on her.

"Cyrus sure does like chocolate cake," Tommy said.

"Did he tell you that?" Annie gave up on the comb and grabbed the hair dryer from the second drawer of her vanity. Tommy was always telling her something Cyrus had said. She sometimes thought the two of them had a language of their own.

"No, but he ate it real fast. Wasn't it s'posed to be my birthday cake?"

Tommy's birthday was on Friday. Annie had made the cake early to freeze in an effort to be a step ahead of herself. She dropped the blow-dryer on the sink counter, grabbed her son's hand and bolted down the stairs. "Cyyyyrus!"

With Tommy still attached to her hand, she skidded to a stop in the kitchen doorway, a run popping up in the right heel of her stockings. Too late. In the middle of the floor sat Cyrus, all one-hundred-plus pounds of him, his nose looking as if it had been dipped in chocolate, the plastic plate on which the cake had been sitting as clean as if it had gone through the dishwasher's pot-scrubber cycle.

"Oh, Cyrus."

"See, Mama. I told you he liked it."

"Bad, Cyrus. At least you look guilty," Annie said, picking up the plate. Chocolate. The cake had been chocolate. Wasn't chocolate bad for dogs? She struggled to remember what she'd heard about it, but only came up with the vague recollection that it could damage their nervous systems.

Annie's own nervous system was well on its way to meltdown.

Cyrus hung his head and plopped down on the floor with a whine. Whether it was guilt or the beginnings of the stomachache that was his destiny, Annie didn't know.

"Is Cyrus sick, Mommy?"

Worry lines knitted her son's forehead. Six-year-old boys shouldn't have worry lines. But more often than not, Tommy did.

"I don't know, honey. He'll probably have a bel-lyache."

"He's not gonna die, is he?" The lines on Tommy's forehead deepened.

Alarm jangled along Annie's spine. Cyrus was Tommy's best friend. As much as she had been against getting the dog, she had to admit he had been good for her son at a time when he'd desperately needed a diversion. But then if J.D. hadn't run off with his all but jail-bait girlfriend, Tommy would have no need for a diversion.

Giving a five-year-old boy a St. Bernard puppy was just the kind of thing J.D. was famous for. At least in the context of their marriage. Tommy had seen one in a dog-food commercial and asked his father if he could have a puppy like that. J.D. had gone right out and bought him one. Of course, doing so had made him a king in Tommy's eyes. And when Annie had said he couldn't keep it, she'd been tossed the mantle of Cruella DeVil.

Considering that Tommy had only recently begun to show signs of the carefree child he had once been, she did not want to risk a setback brought on by Cyrus's sudden demise. And on top of that, Annie now loved him, too. Even if he had been a present from J.D.

"No, honey," she reassured him. "But we'll run him over to Doc Angle's. They'll know what to do."

The cordless phone on the kitchen counter rang, rattling Annie's already rattled nerves. She glared at it, then yanked it up and barked a hello stern enough to deter even the most hardened of the telemarketers who always seemed to call around dinnertime.

"Hey, babe."

Annie dropped her forehead onto a palm and rubbed the heel of her hand against a budding migraine. She really did have to get caller ID. "I do not have time to talk to you, J.D."

Tommy glanced up, his eyes widening in happiness just before a mask of indifference slipped up to conceal it. It had been months since he'd asked to speak to his daddy on the rare occasions that J.D. called. Annie's heart throbbed with the realization that pride demanded this lack of concern even in a boy his age. She and Tommy both had made excuses for J.D. until they'd been forced to admit that was all they were. Excuses.

She turned around so that her back was to Tommy. He got up and trudged into the living room with Cyrus lumbering behind him.

"So the little mayor's staying busy, huh?"

The amusement behind the words made Annie wish for a voodoo doll with extra pins. Divorce rule number 54: ignore jabs deliberately meant to rile. "What do you want, J.D.?"

"What are you offering?"

Annie balked at the flirtation underlining the question. He was amazing. Truly amazing. "J.D." she said, her voice sub-zero.

"To see my son. That's what I want. Put Tommy

on a plane and send him out here to visit, sugar-pie. I miss him.''

The command was issued with all the certainty of a man who never entertained even the notion of the word no. ''I am not sending Tommy across the country by himself, J.D. He's six years old, for heaven's sake!''

''Kids ride airplanes by themselves all the time, Annie,'' J.D. said in the same you're-being-ridiculous voice he'd perfected when they'd been married, and she'd tried to explain why he couldn't just write checks off their bank account without ever looking to see if they had the funds to cover them. ''I have a right to see my son.''

''You know where your son lives, and if you want to see him, you can get on an airplane and come here.'' The last two words took a leap toward hysteria, and she forced herself to draw in a calming breath before going on in a lowered voice. ''You've made no effort to see him in nearly a year, J.D. Do you think you can saunter back into his life as if you just saw him yesterday? How am I supposed to explain that to him?''

''JaaayyyyyDeeeee, I'm still waiting,'' a woman's voice called in the background.

There. She had her explanation. Annie stomped across the kitchen floor and slammed the phone into its wall cradle, hoping the collision would blow a hole in J.D.'s faithless eardrum. But it did little more than rocket a bolt of pain straight up her arm where it landed in the center of the headache now pounding full force.

There had been a time since the demise of their twelve-year marriage when she would have shed a kitchen sink full of tears over that very audible reminder of her husband's betrayal. But even had she cared to indulge the tradition, she didn't have time for it tonight. She glanced at her watch. In twenty minutes, Jack Corbin would be waiting for her at Walker's. Jack Corbin, who hadn't been back to Macon's Point since his father's funeral six years ago, and who, according to Mary Louise Carruthers at the post office, traveled to exotic-sounding places such as St. Tropez, Lyon and San Gimignano (none of which had sounded all that exotic under Mary Louise's pronunciation).

His track record for changing addresses rivaled even J.D.'s.

Annie's stomach churned.

Somehow, she, pinch-hitter Mayor Annie McCabe, former housewife, a woman unable to figure out how to keep her husband from straying, had to persuade a man with enough money to live out the rest of his days on some private island sipping piña coladas, not to give Corbin Manufacturing the death knell.

And before she got around to that, all she had to do was finish drying her hair, change her blouse, drop her son off at the baby-sitter's and deliver Cyrus to the emergency animal hospital. While she was at it, maybe she'd leap a tall building or two just for good measure.

JACK CORBIN PULLED INTO the parking lot of Walker's Restaurant a few minutes before seven. He cut the engine to the Carrera, and it let out a throaty rumble before going silent.

September twilight gave the near-night sky a rosy glow. An easy breeze fanned the leaves of a giant old beech tree that hugged the right side of the building. Jack had ridden his bike by there the morning Mr. Walker had planted that tree. He must have been eight or nine years old then. He'd stopped to ask what kind it was, and Mr. Walker had told him when the tree grew up it would have roots that looked like gnarled old feet. They did, indeed.

Jack ran a palm across a cheek badly in need of a shave, then reached for his cell phone and punched in his office number.

"Corbin, Mitchell Consulting. Pete Mitchell here."

"Hey, Pete."

"You make it out to the boonies?"

"Just got here. And if you weren't from Arkansas, I'd be offended."

Pete laughed. "Fair enough. I just got an e-mail from Fogelman in London a little while ago. Wanted to know when you were coming. I told him you were going to be held up for a week or two. They're anxious for you to get there. But if I had a business in that kind of shape, I'd be anxious, too."

"Actually, I do have a business in that kind of shape. I just don't plan to keep it."

"Auction's all set?"

"Yep. Wish I could snap my fingers and have it be over."

"It's a bummer, that's for sure. Maybe this London stint will be good for you. British babes and—"

"Fogelman breathing down my neck?"

"That's the needle across the record. 'Fraid he comes with the deal. It was a lucrative one so suck it up."

"I knew there was a reason I asked you to be a partner in this firm."

"Pep talks-r-us."

"Everybody's gotta be good for something," Jack said, reaching for the notepad he kept in the center console and scribbling a reminder to e-mail Fogelman his best guess on when he would be arriving.

"So you've got the big meeting with the mayor tonight?"

"During which I'll try to convince her that even after forty-seven phone calls, I haven't changed my mind. And I'm not going to."

"Have to give her an A for persistence."

"Or aggravation."

Pete chuckled. "Wonder if she's hot."

"Do you ever get your mind wrapped around any other subject?"

"I try to discourage it. You'd do well to borrow the philosophy."

"Out of the market."

"When are you going to quit beating yourself up about that, Jack? Lots of people change their mind about getting married. Better before than after."

"At the altar though?"

"Okay, so right before."

"Which makes me a very bad cliché."

"No. Just a man who hasn't found the right woman."

Jack aimed the subject in another direction. "I left a file on my desk with some info I need for the lawyers on the auction. How about scanning it and e-mailing it to me?"

"Not a problem. They have phone jacks down there?"

"Watch it."

"Do it before I leave."

"Check in with you tomorrow." Jack hit the end button on his phone, dropped it on the passenger seat.

Another car pulled up beside him. A man and woman got out, fortyish, headed for the restaurant holding hands. She dropped her head back and laughed at something the man said, her hair brushing her shoulders. A single glimpse of the two made it clear they were a couple of long standing, their ease with one another nearly tangible. A pang of envy hit Jack in the chest, surprising him with its lingering sting. Ironic considering that a year and a half ago, he'd broken off his engagement to a perfectly nice woman because in the end, he hadn't been able to go against his own belief that it wouldn't last.

Jack got out of the car, closed the door with a solid ka-chunk. He crossed the parking lot, fighting with the knot of his tie. What was he doing here, anyway? In addition to the pile of work stacked up on his desk back in D.C., he had about a thousand loose ends to tie up in Macon's Point before he could leave for London. He'd driven straight down, still in his work clothes. What he wanted was a good hot shower, a pair of jeans and a T-shirt. At least the meeting wouldn't last long. He'd say his piece and be on his way.

Walker's hadn't changed much. Looked the same, in fact, except for the fresh coat of paint dolling up the exterior.

Jack pushed open the front door and stepped inside the well-lit foyer where a waitress greeted him with a bright smile that seemed a watt or two above just-friendly. "Welcome to Walker's."

"Thanks. Any chance of getting a table in the back?"

"Shouldn't be a problem," she said, holding up a pink-tipped finger. "Let me just go see."

The place was jam-packed with the dinner crowd. Several heads turned to send him a curious glance. Sudden awkwardness grabbed him by the throat. His name wasn't going to be a popular one around Macon's Point. No doubt about it.

He turned his back to the dining room and shoved

his hands deep in the pockets of his gray wool pants, his gaze resting on the vehicles in the lot outside. His stomach did a hungry rumble, the smells wafting out from the kitchen tempting and familiar. Homemade yeast rolls. Coffee brewing behind the counter. His mother had brought him here when he was a boy more times than he could count, to pick up his father's favorite peach pie on the way home from a visit in town or a dozen chocolate chip cookies for the jar on the kitchen counter. And the three of them had come here for lunch on Sundays when Jack had been in from school. The recollection was poignant, painful.

"Got that table for you."

The waitress was back, beckoning for him to follow her. Her walk had a seismic wave to it, her hips sending the ruffle at the hem of her skirt left to right like the pendulum on a grandfather clock. "I'm Charlotte," she threw over her shoulder. "You sure do look familiar."

"One of those faces." He somehow knew that if she put a name with it, everyone else in the place would soon do the same.

Stopping at the table, Charlotte cocked a hip. "Now there I'd have to disagree. We don't see too many faces like yours around here. You new in town?"

"Not really. Just back for a quick visit."

"Hope you decide to make it a longer one," she

said, adding a not-so-subtle wink to the assertion. "What can I get you to drink?"

"Sweet tea."

"Southern roots." She gave him a nod of approval. "Back in a gnat's blink, honey."

Again, Jack felt the glances being sent his way from the crowded dining room, most less than friendly. He heard his name mentioned once or twice.

"Have you had time to decide?" Charlotte, true to her word, came right back, placed his tea in front of him, righting the lemon wedge teetering on the rim.

"I'm waiting for someone," he said.

"That figures," she said, not bothering to hide her disappointment. "The good ones are always waiting. Just let me know when you're ready." She sauntered off then with a regretful smile.

Jack reached for a couple packs of sugar and emptied them into the glass. This was a mistake. Why hadn't he just called Annie McCabe and cancelled this meeting? Even if he hadn't had his own reasons for wanting to close this chapter of his life once and for all, Corbin Manufacturing was beyond saving. The company hadn't made a penny since his father died. In fact, it had been losing increasingly large sums of money for the past six years.

Ironic, really, that Jack had built a career around fixing broken businesses. Going into hopeless situations, finding the terminal wound from which a company's lifeblood was seeping, and figuring out how to suture it up again.

But in this situation, there was no point in trying to determine a cause when he had no intention of fixing it.

Corbin Manufacturing's demise was inevitable, whether he put it out of its misery by sticking it on the auction block as he fully intended to do, or let it die the slow death it had been dying for years.

CHAPTER TWO

LATE AND FRAZZLED, Annie pulled into the lot at Walker's and parked her car beside a black Porsche that stood out among the other vehicles like a woman in a ballgown at a barbecue. Five dollars said it was his.

"Mama, are you sure Cyrus is gonna be all right?"

"You heard Doc Angle, Tommy. Cyrus will spend the night at the hospital, and we'll pick him up in the morning. He'll be fine."

"Do I get another cake?" he asked, beeps sounding from the handheld Nintendo game he had talked her into letting him bring. Maybe it would at least keep him occupied while she talked to Mr. Corbin of the black Porsche. Her bias against the car was personal. At one time, J.D. had owned three, red, white and blue. Patriotic, at least.

"Absolutely." She flipped open the driver's side vanity mirror and gave herself a critical perusal in the waning light. Her lipstick had somehow worked its way to the corner of one lip. She dug inside her purse for a tissue and rerouted the errant color. She tucked her hair behind her ears and wriggled her skirt around so that the zipper was where it was supposed to be.

She'd managed to get Cyrus to the animal hospital. But her hair was still damp, and the missing button on her blouse had not been replaced, concealed, at least, beneath her jacket.

Far from perfect, but it would have to do. She darted a glance at the dashboard clock. Fifteen minutes late. Not good. This was not good. After all but begging the man's lawyer for a meeting, this was not the impression she'd intended to make. She slid out of the vehicle and ran around to Tommy's door where she unbuckled his seat belt.

"Are we meeting Aunt Clarice?" he asked, hopping out of the car, his gaze still laser-focused on the game.

"No, honey. Mama has a business dinner. Normally, you would have stayed at the sitter's, but we ran out of time because of Cyrus."

"Oh. What's a bizness dinner?"

"It's when people meet in a restaurant and talk about business," Annie said, taking Tommy's hand and hurrying toward the front door of Walker's, her heels refusing to cooperate with the gravel parking lot. Not a brilliant answer, but it seemed to satisfy him. Making a quick vow to do better with the next question her son asked her, Annie attempted to collect her thoughts. She'd intended to be prepared for her meeting with Corbin, to have all her arguments neatly lined up in her head. Facts and figures. Names of people who'd been with the factory thirty years or more. So much for that. She felt as if someone had set up an industrial-size fan inside her brain, and there wasn't a well-planned argument in sight.

Inside the restaurant, Charlotte Turner greeted them, waving a menu at Annie. "Hello, Mayor McCabe," she said with amused emphasis on the mayor part of the greeting. Annie half expected the woman to ruffle her hair and offer up an "Aren't you cute?" to go with it. But then her attitude was no surprise. The biggest part of the town thought Annie's stepping in as a replacement for her husband was one of those things to chuckle about over coffee and a doughnut at the Krispy Kreme.

"How are you, Charlotte?" Annie asked with a deliberately sincere smile.

"Fine. Busy. Hello, Tommy," she said, bending down to tweak his cheek and lift his glasses from his nose. "If you're not the spittin' image of your daddy. Without the specs, of course."

Tommy's smile fell. He hated wearing glasses. The comparison to his father, however, appeared to lessen the blow, temporarily suspending Annie's desire to pour the contents of the water pitcher sitting by the register on top of Charlotte's set-once-a-week hairdo.

"You gonna play baseball like him when you get big?" Charlotte asked.

Tommy nodded with absolute certainty.

Annie bit back a grimace. She took Tommy's hand and said, "I'm meeting someone for dinner. He's probably already here."

"Tall, dark, mysterious-looking as heck?" Before

Annie could reply, Charlotte pointed toward the back and said, "That who you looking for?"

The man wasn't facing the door. Annie had no idea what he looked like. "Maybe."

Charlotte shook her head and said, "No wonder you didn't mind taking over as mayor, Annie. If this is the kind of thing you get to do, I might just run myself next term." A big wink followed the assertion.

Not trusting herself to respond, Annie put a hand on Tommy's shoulder and steered him toward the back of the restaurant, waving at familiar faces as she wound her way through the tables.

She stopped at the booth Charlotte had pointed out. "Mr. Corbin?"

The man stood. "Mayor McCabe?"

Annie nodded, momentarily struck mute. Charlotte Turner might need sensitivity training when it came to little boys, but she was right on this. Annie would never have put a face this good-looking on a man who was about to do to Macon's Point what this one was about to do. In her mind's eye, she'd penciled in something much more weasel-like, sinister, even. And, yes, he did look like the kind of guy who would drive a black Porsche, or closer still, head up the ad campaign for one. He had dark brown hair and the kind of lean, high-cheekboned face that spoke of good genetics and an athletic lifestyle. "I, ah, I hope you don't mind, but my son Tommy is joining us for dinner. Tommy, this is Mr. Corbin."

"H'lo," Tommy said, staring at the man with open curiosity.

"Hello, Tommy," he said, looking, to his credit, only a little taken aback. "It's nice to meet you."

"We had a little emergency at home," Annie said, "and I didn't have time to get him to the sitter's."

"Nothing serious, I hope?"

She shook her head. "Oh, no. Just a St. Bernard, a chocolate cake and a trip to the vet's."

He nodded as if he understood, but Annie suspected she might as well have spouted off a paragraph of Greek for all he would understand of that. Her own life was an unending series of such events, and for one un-maternal moment, she wondered what it would be like to have arrived on time with her hair dry and all her buttons in place.

"May I take your coat?" he asked.

"Thank you," she said, feeling a little awkward as she slipped her arms free of the heavy garment and then helped Tommy slip out of his. He took both coats and hung them on the rack a few feet from their table.

"Please, sit down," he said. "I went ahead and ordered some iced tea. May I ask the waitress to bring you both something?"

His manners surprised her. J.D. had been used to having other people scurry to do things for him, open a door, "Take your coat, Mr. McCabe?" As for Annie, she'd gotten used to doing things for herself. Hanging up her own coat. Ordering her own drink.

"Your tea looks good, actually."

"Can I have hot choc'late?" Tommy piped in.

"May you have hot chocolate," Annie automatically corrected. "And yes, you may."

"One iced tea and one hot chocolate coming right up," Jack Corbin said and went off to tell the waitress. Annie helped Tommy climb onto the booth seat, waited while he scooted toward the wall, then sat down herself.

Corbin was back in less than a minute, sliding into the other side of the booth. Before Annie could say a word, Tommy raised his gaze from his Nintendo game and said, "We're gonna talk bizness."

Unexpected though it was, the comment served as an effective icebreaker. The man across the table smiled and said, "So we are, but why don't we order our dinner first?" He pulled three menus from the stand next to the wall and handed one to them.

"I can't read," Tommy said, but appeared impressed that it had been assumed he could.

"Maybe your mom can take a look at it then."

"Sure, honey," Annie said, anxious to decide on something so she could focus on her speech. "Let's find something you'll like. How about the macaroni and cheese?"

"Uh-uh."

Annie ran her finger down the list of tonight's specials. "Mashed potatoes?"

Tommy shook his head again, this time with more emphasis.

"A hamburger?"

Another headshake.

"How about some soup?"

"No."

Annie heard the dissatisfaction in her son's voice, recognizing where it was headed. For the most part, Tommy was an angel of a child. But ever since J.D. had left, temper tantrums had become a way of life. There was no predicting them, and Tommy's counselor had told her that she should simply let them run their course, that they were the boy's way of punishing her for the changes since his father had left. Another notch on life's belt of unfairness since J.D. had made that decision all by himself, without any help from her.

"Okay," she said in a reasoning tone, praying that she could head this off, "how about a grilled cheese?"

"No," he said, his voice growing louder.

This was not going at all as planned. Sitting across from her was the man who held the fate of this town in the palm of his hand. Annie figured she had one chance and one chance only to get him to at least consider not selling Corbin Manufacturing, and how on earth was she going to do that with Tommy throwing a fit beside her?

"You know what my favorite thing here was when I was your age, Tommy?" Corbin's question was casual.

Tommy looked up, no doubt intrigued that a man

as big as the one sitting in front of them could ever have been his age. "What?"

"Pancakes."

"For supper?"

"For anytime. In fact, I think that's what I'll have tonight."

Tommy pondered that for a moment, then looked at Annie and said, "Can I get pancakes, Mama?"

"May you have them. And yes, you may," Annie said. In another less-than-admirable motherhood moment, she would have let him order jelly beans if that's what it took to head off the storm about to erupt.

Tommy went back to his game, his bad mood dissipating as quickly as it had started.

Annie breathed a silent sigh of relief. "Thank you for your patience, Mr. Corbin. I realize this isn't what—"

"It's Jack. And this is fine."

Jack, then. His response wasn't the one she would have expected. Her own self-painted portrait of Jack Corbin, playboy extraordinaire, did not include the ability to deter little boys from temper tantrums with the finesse of a conductor leading an orchestra through Beethoven's *Fifth*. Guys who drove Porsches didn't do that, did they?

Charlotte appeared then with their drinks, an iced tea for Annie and a hot chocolate with an extra bowl of marshmallows on the side for Tommy.

"Another of your favorites?" Annie asked, surprised and more than a little appreciative.

"Hot chocolate's nothing without the marshmallows."

Annie had no doubt that Jack Corbin had just moved up another level in Tommy's estimation. Next to chocolate cake, marshmallows ruled.

"Careful now. It's hot," Annie warned while Tommy filled the cup with as many of the gooey treats as it would hold.

"What can I get for you?" Charlotte asked. "I'll take you first, Mayor."

Food was the last thing Annie wanted, so she said the first thing that came to mind. "A tossed salad, please. Thousand island on the side."

"All right." Charlotte scribbled on her pad. "And the gentlemen?"

"We're having pancakes," Jack Corbin said as seriously as if he'd just ordered the two of them the best steaks on the menu.

Tommy beamed.

Charlotte looked at Annie and said, "Unpredictable, too? Two stacks of pancakes coming right up."

As soon as she'd headed off toward the kitchen with their order, Tommy said, "Do people always get to order pancakes when they talk about bizness?"

"Not always," Jack said. "But I'd have to say it's a pretty good idea."

Annie smiled and smoothed down a wayward strand of Tommy's hair. Her son had managed to defuse some of the nervousness she would have no doubt been feeling had she been here alone with Jack Corbin. She'd been lucky to get the man to meet her at all, and she couldn't afford to waste any more of the limited time she had to make her case.

"Jack." She cleared her throat and willed her nerves to settle. "I know I mentioned this in my letters and calls to your attorney—"

"All of them?" he interrupted.

Was he teasing her? The thought tripped her up a bit. "Ah, yes, I'm sure. I would like to reiterate again just how much Macon's Point would like to see Corbin Manufacturing remain in business. A great many of the people who live here rely on your factory for their—"

"My daddy's famous."

The announcement came from Tommy who had looked up from his game and was waiting for a reaction.

"He is?" Jack asked with a raised eyebrow. "What's he do?"

"He plays baseball."

"Tommy, honey, Mr. Corbin and I are discussing—"

"For what team?"

"He used to be with the Braves, but he got hurt."

"Is your daddy J. D. McCabe?"

Tommy nodded, so proud that Annie's heart hurt.

"He is famous," Jack said, looking impressed

enough to make Tommy light up again. "He's quite a player."

"I want to be just like him when I get big. He lives in Los—" Tommy hesitated and then looked up at Annie. "Where is it, Mama?"

"Los Angeles, honey."

"Mama and Daddy are divorced, so he has to live out there."

"Oh," Jack said, the response admirably neutral.

Annie drew in a quick breath, put a hand on her son's hair and said, "Tommy, we'll have to tell Mr. Corbin about Daddy's baseball career another time. We can't keep him here all night, and he and I have some very important things to discuss."

"Do you like baseball, Mr. Corbin?" Tommy asked, completely ignoring Annie's attempt at reason.

"I like to watch it, but I never was very good at playing it."

Tommy considered this for a moment, and then said, "Not everybody can be a great baseball player."

Annie recognized the words her son had used in an attempt to console Jack. They were the same ones she'd used since Tommy had first started asking her if she thought he'd grow up to be a great baseball player like his father. One of her greatest fears was that Tommy would hinge his sense of self-worth on whether or not he could play like J.D., and this was the last thing she wanted for him. "Tommy, honey—"

"You're right about that," Jack said. "Everyone is born with different strengths and abilities."

Tommy considered this for a brief moment. "What's yours?"

Jack rubbed a hand around the back of his neck and said, "Hmm. I guess I would say I might have a talent for putting things back together again."

Annie could see that the comment was as intriguing to her six-year-old son as it was to her.

"Like puzzles?" Tommy asked.

"Sort of, but with real-life situations."

"Oh."

Tommy let it go, and for once Annie wished her son would persist with another question.

Charlotte appeared with their dinners.

"Let's see, one tossed salad for our mayor," she said, placing the bowl of lettuce and vegetables in front of Annie. "And for our boys, pancakes."

She set the loaded plates in front of "the boys," bestowing a there-you-are-sugar on Tommy and then landing a what-do-you-say-we-meet-up-later smile on Jack Corbin.

"Mama, will you cut up my pancakes?"

"Sure, honey." Annie darted a glance at Jack who was waiting politely for the two of them to begin eating. "Go ahead, please," she said.

He reached for the syrup bottle and poured liberally until his plate was a pond with the pancakes floating in the center like a stack of lily pads.

"Can I have as much syrup as Mr. Corbin, Mama?"

Annie tried not to smile. "I'll pour, and you say when, okay?"

Jack passed the syrup bottle to her with a slightly embarrassed shrug, which startled her with its unexpected appeal. "Okay, so in some ways, a man never grows up."

"In most ways," Annie said, the remark slipping out before she had given it an edit.

He cocked an eyebrow and passed up commenting on that, but Annie didn't miss the curiosity in his eyes.

After finishing with Tommy's pancakes, Annie drizzled dressing across her salad, took a few token bites and then put down her fork, feeling as if the lettuce were sticking in her throat. The sooner she said what she'd come to say, the sooner the knot of nerves inside her would dissolve. "As I was saying, Jack—" She stopped, cleared her throat, then tried again. "Five hundred people in this town will be out of work if you close down your factory. That means they won't be able to pay their mortgages or car payments. They will be without health insurance. If you shut down that factory, you might as well shut down the whole town."

She'd gained momentum near the end, strong and not a little accusatory. Annie happened to believe that every word she had just said was true, and she somehow needed to make him understand that. "There must be something that can be done. It's not as if the company is in bankruptcy."

Jack Corbin studied her for several long seconds. Annie resisted the distinct urge to fidget under that level stare and remained still in her seat. It was the most intimidating stare she'd ever faced in her life. *Don't look away, Annie. If you do, he wins.*

"Close enough," he said, a glimmer of respect in his eyes when he said, "Look, Mrs. McCabe—"

"Annie."

"Annie," he inclined his head, "I appreciate your position. And I'm sorry that things have ended this way. My father's company provided the people of this town with livelihoods for a lot of years. But he's not here anymore. And Corbin Manufacturing was his vision, not mine."

Annie's heart sank. As explanations went, his sounded as if it had been forged in steel. The set look to his jaw told her that she didn't have an icicle's chance in Tahiti of turning this particular situation around. She suddenly felt tired and resigned and downright sad.

Some combination of those emotions must have been reflected in her face. He sighed and said, "Look, I appreciate the difficulty of your position, Annie. I hope you can do the same of mine."

Annie toyed with a piece of lettuce at the edge of her bowl, avoiding his gaze. She looked up then and met it head on. "Actually, I can't. You see, I know most of these people as individuals. I know Sam

Crawford who works in your finishing department. He
has a wife with MS and three children he's somehow
managing to raise while working and taking care of
her. I know Milly Thomsen who works in the front
office. She's supporting herself and twin girls after
her husband was killed in a logging accident last year.
I see the individual tragedies that will happen in this
town if that factory closes down, and no, I can't accept the rightness of that. Not if there's any way at
all to avoid it.''

Tommy's heels thunked against the lower panel of
the booth. ''I'm sleepy, Mama. Are you done talkin'
bizness?''

''I think we're just about finished, Tommy,'' Jack
said, shifting his unreadable gaze from Annie to her
son who was rubbing his eyes with the back of a fist.

Annie put an arm around Tommy's shoulders, her
heavy heart dropping a few more inches. ''Thank you
for listening. I only wish I could have said something
to make you reconsider.''

She got up from the booth then, pulled her wallet
from her purse and put a twenty on the table. ''Let's
go home, Tommy.''

Tommy blinked with sleepy eyes and said, ''You
didn't eat all your pancakes, Mr. Corbin.''

Jack got up and stood politely to the side. ''No, I
didn't. I wasn't as hungry as I thought.''

''Well, we'll be going,'' Annie said stiffly, taking
Tommy's hand.

''Good night,'' Tommy said.

"Nice to meet you, Tommy."

"Good night," Annie said. She led her son back through the restaurant, the weight of failure heavy on her shoulders.

AFTER LEAVING WALKER'S, Jack followed South Main out of town, winding through the September night, leaving his window cracked to reacquaint himself with the smells of the country. Burning leaves in the front yard of what had once been the old Jefferson house. Corn silage at Saul's Dairy.

He traveled the last two miles of the secondary road that led to Glenn Hall behind a seen-better-days Ford pickup with a missing taillight and a lopsided bumper, the right side of which nearly touched the pavement every time the driver tapped his brakes.

For once, Jack didn't mind the pace. His regular life revolved around being in a hurry. Last-minute trips. Nearly-missed planes. A new city every week. He'd set his life up that way, and most of the time, it suited him just fine. Slowing down gave a man too much time to think, often enough about things that didn't bear up under scrutiny. Like where he'd been instead of where he was going. That he couldn't go back and erase tracks he'd already made. All he could do was point his feet in another direction next time out.

Jack hated letting people down, and it seemed as if lately he'd become an expert at it.

He'd certainly let Annie McCabe down tonight. And he felt like a heel.

Okay, so maybe it hadn't been as easy as he'd expected it to be. Saying no to a woman with eyes the color of Swiss chocolate and a little boy at her side. It had been the most unconventional business meeting Jack had ever attended.

He didn't know what he'd expected in Annie, maybe forty-five and frumpy. Nix that image. She was cute like a Meg Ryan where a first glance says, hmm, nice. Second glance, very nice.

She had the kind of mouth that got him distracted fast. Full lower lip which she worried with even, white teeth in between the arguments she'd been launching at him with fastball accuracy.

And she'd been married to J. D. McCabe. J.D. had been a couple years older than Jack. Jack had gone to a private school, so their paths rarely crossed. But he remembered J.D. as a guy with a laser-beam smile and more than his share of confidence. He wondered why the idea of Annie with him didn't quite gel.

The truck in front of him slowed to a crawl, then angled right and rolled off down a gravel driveway, freeing up the road. Jack nudged the accelerator to the floor, suddenly anxious to knock out each of the obligations standing between him and tying up for good these last connections to Macon's Point.

The Porsche raced up the next hill, rounded a curve, and there it was. Glenn Hall. The car's headlights arced across two enormous fieldstone columns marking the entrance to the farm his father had left to Daphne Corbin, his second wife. Now Jack's by default.

He stopped and got out to open the gate with the key his attorney had sent him. He swung the gate arms wide. A three-quarter moon backlit a white four-rail fence in need of paint. Standing beneath an old maple some twenty feet inside the pasture were two big Percheron horses gazing at him with open curiosity.

Jack ducked back inside the Porsche and found two pieces of peppermint candy in the glove compartment. He crossed the driveway to the fence. One of the horses nickered and ambled over.

"Hey, Sam," Jack said, unwrapping the candy and giving it to him. "Still the brave one, I see."

The other horse edged up beside them, not quite as courageous, but unwilling to be left out. "Hey, Ned, old boy." Jack gave him the candy and rubbed his forehead. Both horses stood there, crunching their candy and sniffing Jack's arm.

Just the sight of them cut off the air in his lungs, flooding him with vivid memories of his father. Hooking up the team on a Sunday afternoon, taking Jack and his mother for a wagon ride down the old country roads surrounding the farm. To most people, this side of Joshua Corbin had never meshed with the image of a CEO whose business provided a big percentage of the town's jobs. But to Jack, it had. As a little boy, it was seeing his father drive those gigantic horses that had made his heart swell with pride, made him want to tell the world that was his father up there. He'd taught Jack a lot about life through those horses. How to care for things that depended on you. That a soft voice brought about the desire to please in a way a harsh hand never could.

They were old now. In their late twenties at least. There had been four at one time. He threw a glance across the pasture behind him. If the other two had been out there grazing, they would have made their way to the fence already. He was surprised any of them were still alive, more so that Daphne hadn't sold them all long ago. He almost wished she had just so he didn't have to.

Sam and Ned had spent their entire lives here. He'd find a good home for them, but that didn't make him feel any better.

He gave them a last rub, got back in the car and followed the winding driveway to the house that sat on a slight rise some quarter mile away. From the outside, at least, nothing had changed. The house had been built from fieldstone. White wooden shutters bracketed each window. An enormous mahogany door marked the center entrance. Jack's father had built it for his mother, the two of them using an old pickup on weekends to load up the rock for the house from the edges of the fields on the farm. It was she who should have lived here all these years. She who should have left it to him. Not Daphne.

He got out, leaving the couple of bags he'd brought with him in the back of the car.

Jack pulled the key from his pocket and opened the front door. He'd expected to be greeted with the musty scent of neglect. Instead, the house smelled clean, fresh, as if someone had just been through with a bottle of lemon Pledge and a bucket of soapy water.

Jack flicked on a light, then stood in the hallway, giving himself a moment to acquaint memory with reality. He ventured down the front hallway, his footsteps echoing around him. It was a sad, no-one-lives-here sound that did not fit his memories of a childhood rich with all the things that make a house a home. Warm cooking smells. Winter evenings spent in front of a crackling fire. Summer afternoons on the back porch drinking lemonade.

The memories stung.

''Jack?''

He swung around, and there in the doorway stood Essie Poindexter. Rounder than he remembered. But with the same smile that connected in a straight line from her mouth to her eyes.

Emotion had a lock on his throat. ''Essie,'' he finally said.

''Land's sake, I can't believe it's really you, son.''

They stepped forward at the same time, meeting halfway across the room in a fierce hug, he towering over her short, stout frame, she with her chubby arms locked tight about his waist.

When he finally pulled back, tears marked her

round cheeks. He reached out and rubbed them away with his thumbs. She hadn't changed much, a few more lines in her face, maybe, softened, though, by the warm welcome there. The sight of her deluged him with reminders of a childhood in which she had played a more-than-significant part. For as long as he could remember, she had lived in a house his father had built for her at one end of the farm. She'd been hired as a housekeeper to help out Jack's mother, but Jack had always thought of her as family.

"I saw lights coming up the driveway and figured I better see who it was. Thought you could slip in without seeing old Essie, huh?" she asked, the hurt behind the question barely concealed.

He pulled her against his chest again and rubbed her slightly humped back with the palm of his hand. "Of course I was coming to see you, Es."

"I'd say it's about time," she said, pulling away to squint up at him. She stepped farther back and took a longer look. "I remember your father at thirty-three. You look just like him. Handsome as the day is long. I just wish you two had mended your fences."

He held up a hand. "Essie, don't, okay?"

"I expected to see you here for the funeral, son," she said, her words colored with equal doses of admonishment and disappointment. "I know you never got to know her, but she was your stepmother. She was sick for a good while."

"I didn't know. But I'm sorry about it, Essie. I was out of the country when it happened. I didn't receive word until the day after the funeral. Besides, I wouldn't have belonged there, anyway.''

She gave him a look of disagreement, then pressed her lips together as if deciding this wasn't the time to argue. She reached for the cover draped across the closest chair and yanked it off, sending up a puff of dust. ''Give me a couple hours, and I'll have this place looking livable,'' she said, tugging at the sheet on the couch. ''If you'd have let me know you were coming, I'd already have it done.''

''You don't have to do that. I'm only staying a couple nights, Es. That's all.''

Essie didn't say anything for several moments, the sheet in her hands slumping to the floor. ''You're really going through with it then? Selling the factory.''

''It's for the best.''

''For who?'' she asked quietly. ''Surely, not this town.''

''Essie—''

She raised a hand and cut him off. ''I know you think you have your reasons, Jack. And Lord knows at the time, I had a hard time understanding why your father did what he did. But sometimes, you've got to step a little closer for the picture to come into focus.''

''Dad left the business to Daphne when he died. I think that made his feelings pretty clear. If he had wanted me to have it, he would have left it to me. Anyway, I didn't come back to rehash the past,'' he said, the words coming out harsher than he'd intended. Meeting the older woman's sorrowful gaze, he immediately regretted his abruptness.

"Then why did you come back? You could have sold off this place and that business without ever setting foot in this house."

"I know."

"Then why did you?"

"I'm not sure," he answered, his tone softening, honest in this, at least. He'd never been able to lie to Essie. Even at eight when he'd raided the kitchen cookie jar before dinner and had the worst stomachache of his life, he'd owned up.

"Could I ask one thing of you then, son? Don't leave again until you can answer that question for me."

CHAPTER THREE

ON THE OTHER end of the country, J. D. McCabe had spent the better part of the day stewing. Stretched out now on a lounge chair by the swimming pool in his backyard, he muttered a few curses at the fairer gender's inability to see reason.

Dadblame Annie's hide. What in the world had happened to the moldable woman he'd married? There had been a time when he could snap his fingers, and she'd practically run to meet whatever need he needed met.

She was still mad at him for running off with Cassie, that much he knew. But damn it all to hell, two divorced adults ought to be able to work things out in a dignified manner. He wanted to see his son, and she was bending over backward to make sure that didn't happen. He was no dummy. Women had an unbelievable need for revenge when they considered themselves mistreated, and Annie had decided to use their son as her weapon of choice.

Why couldn't she just get over it?

He flipped onto his stomach, reached for the Bloody Mary Cassie had brought out to him a few minutes ago and took a long sip. The generous portion of alcohol she had added to his tomato juice burned a gulch down his throat and lit a simultaneous fire under his already well-stoked indignation. He wasn't going to stand for Annie being so selfish. He had rights. Not to mention he was a celebrity with five commercials running on network TV.

And Tommy was his son. With his genes. His potential to be a great ball player some day.

But not if she brought him up believing ballet was just as admirable as baseball if that was a person's chosen passion.

Let him decide if that's what he wants for himself, J.D.

Wrong! On some things, a child had to be pointed in a certain direction, shoved along a little, if necessary. How the heck was a six-year-old supposed to know what he wanted to do with his life? If J.D. wasn't mistaken, the boy was going to have his daddy's arm. And if Tommy was told he was going to be a great baseball player like his dad, then odds were he would be.

But Annie was so convinced she was right not to push the boy. In his opinion, this was just one more way for her to pay him back. By denying him the chance to see his own talent reflected back in his son.

Who did she think she was? She'd been nothing more than a starry-eyed teenager when he'd met her in Atlanta. He'd given her a life most girls would have run barefoot across nails for a chance at. But of course Annie had never appreciated it. Had always looked at the few negatives of his career. She'd hated the traveling, the moving around. Why had she never seen the excitement in it? Exposure to new things, new people. J.D. thrived on that. And Annie's inability to bend even one iota had been the true cause of the end of their marriage. She could be mad at him until the sun turned blue, but the way he saw it, she was the one at fault for their splitting up, anyway.

And now she wanted to keep him from seeing Tommy.

He let that simmer for a while. Sweat began to bead on his nose, causing his four-hundred-dollar sunglasses to slip. He shoved them back in place.

The problem with Annie was that she'd developed way too big an opinion of herself. Ever since she'd stepped into his shoes as mayor of Macon's Point—his own term as mayor had been little more than an amused diversion while he tried to figure out how to accept that he was never going to play pro baseball again—she'd gotten just a little too big for her britches. She actually thought she was going to make a difference in that podunk town. How much difference did she think she was going to make in a place that was never going to be anything special?

"Are you still fretting over that phone call, honeybee?"

J.D. looked up. Cassie stood at the sliding glass door of their Tuscan contemporary house, peering at him over the rim of her four-hundred-dollar sunglasses, identical to his. Why was it that she wanted them to have matching everything?

She was twenty-two to his thirty-five. That explained a lot of it. Youth left a few blanks for maturity to fill in later on. *Profound, J.D.* He should write that one down in case he got around to penning his memoirs one day.

Cassie's adoration was kind of cute, but if he wasn't careful she'd have him parading around L.A. in matching *I'm Hers, I'm His* T-shirts.

If her youth allowed for a few semi-irritating quirks, it made up for it in other ways. He sent a glance over the strings holding her bikini together in three strategic locations. She had the kind of sex drive that required his presence twice a day. She was damn near about to wear him out. Which was fairly laughable, considering his complaints about the desert-dry sex life he'd had with Annie.

"I'm not fretting," he said, planting his forehead on the chair and staring at the terra-cotta tile beneath.

She click-clacked across the pool deck and squatted down beside him, one hand lacing through his hair. "You are."

"I'm not."

She sighed. "Why don't you just go get him, J.D.? I wouldn't mind having the little sweetkins live here with us. We could hire a nanny. Maybe one from South America. I hear that's all the rage with the better families."

"The courts always rule in favor of the mother on custody, Cass."

She raised an eyebrow and sent him a silly-boy look. "But that's with regular people. You're J. D. McCabe."

A grin broke through his gloom. Cassie might be young, but sometimes she did have a point.

THE DOORBELL RANG at two minutes past six-thirty on Sunday morning.

Clarice. Annie knew it before she pulled back the living-room curtain and saw her sister's green Explorer parked in the driveway. She went to the door in her worn white bathrobe (the one J.D. had called asexual, and she'd therefore kept just as a matter of principle). She opened the door with her hair still sticking out from where she'd slept on it—more like tossed on it—and mascara smudged under her eyes.

"Lovely," came Clarice's raised eyebrow assessment.

"It's still dark outside. Not everyone falls out of bed looking like they're ready for *Star Search*."

Clarice chuckled and sauntered past her, holding up two cups of Krispy Kreme coffee and a paper bag emitting the aroma of glazed doughnuts, her standard offering whenever she showed up on Annie's doorstep at an hour most people would throttle her for. Looking great, of course. Shoulder-length blond hair just tousled enough that it was hard to tell if she'd come straight from bed or a very expensive hair-dresser.

People used words like *striking* to describe Clarice. Clothes looked great on her—all clothes. At thirty-four, Clarice could pull off even the kind that should normally be reserved for twenty and under. If she weren't her sister, Annie could have seriously hated her.

She followed Clarice into the kitchen, wiping a hand over eyes that still felt gritty from lack of sleep.

"So, what? I have to hear from the local grapevine that you were at Walker's last night with the infamous Jack Corbin?"

"I was going to call you this morning."

"You could have called me before."

"So you could have one of your star reporters conveniently located at the next table over? Don't think so."

"Would I ever—"

"Yes."

Clarice laughed, making herself at home on one of the bar stools tucked under the island in the center of Annie's kitchen. "So how'd it go? Have you saved the town yet?"

Annie went to the sink, turned on the faucet and stuck the plate on which Tommy's birthday cake had once perched under the running water. "I'm glad you can see the humor in it. I haven't managed to locate any yet. Because I'm the last person who should be trying to convince Jack Corbin of anything."

Clarice bit into her doughnut, and in a less-than-Clarice-like moment of bad manners, said around a mouthful, "Tell me what you said. What he said."

"I said please. And he said no."

"Annniiieee. The long version if you will."

"He drives a Porsche."

"Hmm." With interest. "What's he look like?"

"Like a guy who drives a Porsche."

"Hmmmm." More interest.

"Clar, you're so deep."

"It's one of my good points." Clarice smiled. "So really. Could you be a little more specific?"

"I don't know. Good-looking."

"A detail or two would be appreciated."

"Dark-brown hair. Nice eyes."

"Fit or soft?"

"Fit."

"Like a runner or a weight lifter?"

"In between."

"Any rings?"

"Didn't notice."

"Did, too."

"Okay, no."

"Hah. So he was good-looking enough for you to look at his ring finger."

Annie rolled her eyes and pulled the doughnut Clarice had brought her out of the bag, taking a bite before elaborating. "Jack Corbin doesn't need that factory or this town. He's made up his mind. It's not much more complicated than that."

"Did you explain how half the town is going to be out of work if he dumps that company?" Clarice's pretty face drew inward with a frown, her doughnut acting as a pointer for accentuation. "How people have mortgages, and car payments and medical bills—" She broke off there, breathless with indignation. This was Clarice the editor talking, the *Star Search* beauty contestant having left the room. This was a woman who would gladly run a four-page expose on every awful thing the man had ever done (provided she could dig it up) if it meant convincing him to reverse his decision.

"I did, Clarice. Specifics, examples, every solid argument I could manage to think of in front of a man eating a stack of pancakes."

"A what?" Clarice's frown lowered a watt or two.

"Pancakes. He ordered pancakes to keep Tommy from having a tantrum."

Clarice pondered that for a moment, then said, "That's odd."

"You mean in keeping with the monster everyone's made him out to be?"

"I didn't say that."

"No, but it's true," Annie said, leaving half her doughnut in the wake of the realization that she'd have to walk into town and back to work off even half those fat grams. She took a sip of her still-hot coffee, adding, "He doesn't have a life here anymore. I can't really blame him for not holding on to the company."

"Yeah, but to dump it at auction, just sell it off piece by piece. That's not right. He could at least wait for a buyer. Then people wouldn't have to lose their jobs."

Ever since she'd left the diner last night, Annie had been unable to shake the sense of failure hanging over her. Yes, she knew how important this was to the town of Macon's Point. She knew how much hardship the company's closing would create. And she felt terrible about it. But the fact was that she, by educational credentials, was barely qualified to work at the Star-Vue Drive-in roller-skating burgers between car windows. She'd finished high school by GED after running off and marrying J.D. at eighteen. She knew a lot about baseball travel schedules, shoulder injuries and fastballs. But not a darn thing about how to save a dying town. "I feel like I've let everybody down, Clar."

Clarice looked up, eyes snapping. "That's ridiculous."

"No, it isn't. I got asked to finish out J.D.'s term because people felt sorry for me. I've never had any illusions that I was qualified for the job, but I wanted to prove that they weren't wrong to offer it to me."

"They weren't wrong."

Annie sighed and took a last sip of her coffee. "Well, after Corbin Manufacturing closes, Macon's Point won't be big enough to need a mayor."

"Aunt Clarice!"

Clarice swung her bar stool around. "Well, hey, sleepyhead, it's about time you got up."

Tommy catapulted into Clarice's arms, nearly sending her over backward on the bar stool. "I didn't know you were here!"

"I came over for an early visit," she said, ruffling his blond hair, which was exactly the same color as hers. "Brought you a doughnut, too," she said, reaching for the bag.

"What kind?"

"Whole wheat," she said, dead serious.

"Yukkkk," Tommy said, making a face.

Clarice laughed. "You know what kind I got you. Blueberry filled, of course."

Tommy grinned. Had it been for anyone other than Clarice, Annie might have been hurt that her son hadn't even noticed she was in the room yet. Tommy adored Clarice. It was mutual. And she couldn't blame him. Clarice doted on her nephew, made him feel special.

"Mama, can I watch a video?"

"Sure, honey."

Tommy took his doughnut and headed for the living room.

"I can't believe I actually thought I could turn this situation around, Clarice. Why did I ever take on this job, anyway?"

"Because you care about this town, and it needs somebody who cares about it." She resumed her position on the bar stool. "So. Here's an idea."

Annie recognized the tone in her sister's voice. Failure did not exist in Clarice's vocabulary. Never had. Never would. "What?" Knowing even as she asked the question that she wasn't going to like the answer.

"Let's go out to see him this morning. Together. I'll go as editor of the county newspaper. You as town mayor. We'll state our case for letting another company buy him out. See if we can get him to at least agree to consider it."

"Oh, Clarice, I don't think—"

"But you don't know. And how can we not at least give it a shot?"

She was right. Annie knew it and couldn't deny it with any real conviction. It was the kind of thing Clarice had always been able to do. Put herself on the line. But then it almost always worked out in her favor. Maybe it would this time as well. In all likelihood, she should have been the one to talk to him in the first place. "You don't think he'll have us thrown off his property?" she asked, half kidding, half not.

"Two babes like us?" Clarice tossed her *Star Search* hair. "I don't think so."

"A MAN COULD get used to living this way."

Essie stood in front of the gas-top Viking range, flipping strips of bacon with a long-handle fork. "You move yourself back in this house, Jack Corbin, and I'll see to it that you do get used to it."

Jack smiled. Lord, he'd missed this woman. Hadn't realized how much until this morning when he'd followed his nose down to the kitchen where she had a pot of the best coffee he'd ever tasted going. Essie's view of the world was one he wished he could bottle and sell. Her face stamped with wrinkles, it was Essie who had long ago taught him the value of a smile. That it opened doors. Made people feel welcome.

Damn shame, then, that he hadn't been able to summon up one last night when Annie McCabe had thanked him in her cool, composed voice, taken her son's hand and left Walker's with an admirable, but unsuccessful, attempt to hide her disappointment. He'd woken up this morning to the nagging feeling that he wanted her to know it wasn't personal. That it had nothing to do with her, but everything to do with him and the fact that he had no intention of cleaning up the mess Daphne had managed to make of his father's business.

He was sure he looked like a monster to her.

And it bothered him.

Movement just past the window caught his eye. Sam, one of the Percherons, stood at the board fence at the edge of the yard, using a post top to reach an itch under his jaw. In the daylight, Jack could see that gray hair had long since threaded its way through the horse's mane, but there was still a dignity to him that made Jack remember how proud his father had been of the team. As proud of those horses as he'd been of the business he'd built from the ground up. A wave of sadness hit him for the fact that they would not live out the rest of their lives here, and for the imminent demise of the furniture business his father had put his life into.

But Jack wasn't responsible for the collapse of the company. Only the decision to let it go. And it was the right decision.

He thought about Annie and the disappointment in her eyes. It *was* the right decision.

Essie set a plate in front of him, covered with enough bacon, eggs and homemade biscuits to feed a family of four. "That's the best-looking meal I've seen in ages," Jack said, turning off the laptop he'd used to download the file Pete had sent him last night. "Aren't you eating, Es?"

"Already did," she said, dropping a frying pan in the sink and reaching for a scrub brush. "You go ahead. Enjoy."

He'd just polished off the last of his bacon when he heard himself asking, "Do you know Annie McCabe, Essie?"

"Everybody knows Annie," Essie said, taking a dish towel to the frying pan she'd just finished scrubbing.

"I met her last night. Seems like a nice woman."

"Maybe too nice. Got herself lassoed into finishing out her ex-husband's term as mayor. Far as I'm concerned, she's done a much better job at it than he ever would have, too. How a man could leave a wife and son like that to run off with some young thing he hadn't known more than a few days—'' Essie broke off there, shaking her head. "I don't understand people anymore. Commitments just don't mean what they used to."

On that Jack had to agree. He'd learned that lesson a long time ago. And yet he'd somehow managed to live his own life as a perfect example of a man unable to commit.

Jack was still thinking about that thirty minutes later over another cup of coffee and the rest of the morning paper. Essie had gone off to do an errand in town. The doorbell rang and he went to answer it.

Annie McCabe stood on his front porch, looking as though she'd rather be anywhere else in the world. Another woman stood next to her, her body language making it clear she was the one who'd brought them here.

"I'm sorry to come by so early," Annie said. "This is—"

"Hi, I'm Clarice Atkins," the other woman interrupted, sticking out a hand. "Annie's sister and editor of the county newspaper. Is there any way we could take up a little of your time this morning?"

Never would have guessed the sisters part. The two women bore no physical resemblance whatsoever. Not even in the way they carried themselves. The world had never said no to the sister.

"Come in," he said, stepping aside and waving them past him. "How about some coffee?"

"We've had our quota, but thank you," Clarice

said. "What a beautiful house. I've admired it so
many times from the road."

"Thanks." He pointed them toward the kitchen,
followed behind, noticing some details of the two:
Annie was three or four inches taller, had full, shoulder-length hair, a sort of sun-dappled blond. Clarice's
hair hung mid-back, the color more along the lines of
Marilyn Monroe. Most interesting, still, the body language. Annie, looking as if she'd been dragged here.
Clarice, pretty sure she was going to get what she
came for.

In the kitchen, they stood for a moment, he not
exactly sure what was expected of him.

"Lovely view," Clarice said, looking out the big
kitchen window where Sam was still hanging out by
the fence. "What kind of horses?"

"Percherons. They were my father's. Retired
now."

"My, they're big. Like the ones in the beer commercial?"

"Those are Clydesdales, aren't they?" This from
Annie.

Jack nodded.

"They're beautiful," Annie said. "Did your father
drive them?"

"Four in hand. He had two more at one time."

"I bet that was something to see."

"It was," Jack said, surprised by the long-tamped-
down pride for his father that rose up to color the
admission.

He looked at Annie, and their gazes held in a moment of something he would have been hard-pressed to put a label on. Surprised him with the vague regret that he had not met her under circumstances where he wasn't set up to play the role of bad guy.

"I—we wanted to invite you to a picnic," Annie said, no longer looking directly at him. "Tuesday afternoon at the factory. Kind of a farewell thing the employees are having. Everyone's bringing a dish."

He remembered then that he had liked her voice last night. Soft blurs on the end of certain words giving away the fact that she'd spent a good part of her life in the South.

He folded his arms across his chest, leaned against the kitchen counter, and put that realization back in the drawer labeled *inappropriate* where it belonged. "Seems like I'd be the last person they'd want there."

"Seems that way," she agreed. "But they might surprise you. And it would give you a chance to put faces to the process."

That last part was thrown out as a challenge. He'd expected the sister to be the one coming at him with a few sharp knives, but so far she was letting Annie do the job. He didn't miss the underlying accusation. If you're going to take away the livelihood of all those people, you could at least know who they are.

And he wouldn't back down. She was right. He had no problem standing behind his decision, especially in front of the people who worked at Corbin Manufacturing. This was a business decision, and as far as they were concerned, nothing personal about it.

"When does it start?"

"Five-thirty." Clarice now. "We could swing by and pick you up if you like."

Surprise flickered across Annie's face and then disappeared behind a veil of casual agreement. She would not have issued that invitation, Jack knew. "Thanks, but I've got my car," he said, sparing her.

Her relief was visible, and he found himself vaguely unsettled by the realization that Annie didn't care to spend any more time with him than she had to.

"Okay, then," she said, in a let's-go-now tone of voice. "We'll look for you on Tuesday."

"What should I bring?"

"Just yourself would be fine," Clarice said, the surface of the reply nothing more than a polite answer, but if Jack wasn't mistaken, there was subtle flirtatiousness beneath.

"Whatever you'd like," Annie said, a strait-laced reply that made her sister's stand out in stark contrast.

"I'll see what I can rustle up."

CHAPTER FOUR

"I. WANT. HIM."

Clarice made her dazed declaration with Glenn Hall still framed in the rearview mirror of Annie's Tahoe.

Annie accelerated, and a cloud of dust kicked up behind them on the gravel driveway. "Clarice," she said in her best you-know-better voice.

"I know. I'm not supposed to like him."

"I didn't say that," Annie objected. "It's just that a lot is riding on whether or not he changes his mind."

"Agreed. Point being?"

"Point being that needs to be our focus."

"You afraid that steering wheel's going somewhere?"

"What?" Annie looked down at her own white-knuckled grip, immediately loosened it. "I guess I feel a lot of pressure on this, Clarice. It's important."

"Well, I know that. But what harm can come from me showing a little interest in him?"

"I don't know. Just that maybe it's not a good time to distract him."

"There are distractions, and there are distractions."

It was pointless to argue. Annie knew her sister well enough to recognize immediate infatuation when it struck.

Clarice popped on a pair of black Armani sunglasses, slid down in her seat and blew out a sigh. "Sorry I was zero help in there. But mercy, I have never in my life seen a man that good-looking."

"You think?" Annie shot some deliberate neutrality into her response. Clarice hardly needed encouragement.

"Think? You're kidding, right?" Disbelief reverberated through the Tahoe's interior. "Annie, surely J.D. didn't do that much damage to your eligible man antennae."

"Mine's on temporary hiatus in the hall closet."

Clarice laughed. "At least you can joke about it now."

"They call that progress in therapy circles."

"Well, it is, actually. For a long time, I couldn't bring myself to say his name because it hurt too much to see the pain on your face."

The mood in the Tahoe had gone suddenly somber. Annie heard the love in her sister's voice and was grateful for it. Clarice had indeed seen her on the down side of disillusion. Not a pretty sight. "I have a feeling J.D. and Jack Corbin have a lot in common."

Clarice's perfectly arched eyebrows shot toward the roof. "How so?"

"Self-interest being their number one priority."

"Well, I won't deny it where J.D. is concerned. But isn't it jumping the gun to hang that sign in Jack Corbin's window just yet?"

Annie kept her gaze on the road, maneuvered around a brown bag in the middle of her lane that had fallen off the A&E Seed truck in front of them. Guilt needled at her. Maybe it was a tad unfair. She was going on surface impressions, after all. Hadn't she been the one defending him to Clarice just a couple of hours ago? And now she was ready to put him in the same box with J.D. and toss the key in Lake Heron. "I just wish he would give the company a chance to get on its feet. That's all."

"Maybe he will. Party's not over yet. And even though I talked a big game before going over there this morning, I wimped. But I've got all the googly-eyed stuff out of the way now, so maybe I'll actually be able to string together a few coherent sentences at the picnic."

Annie smiled.

"You aren't interested in him, are you?" Clarice asked, failing to hide her worry.

"Oh, Clarice, of course not," Annie said. As sisters, they'd had this conversation numerous times in their lives. And Annie always said the same thing because if Clarice really wanted the guy, she didn't stand a chance, anyway. Not that she was interested in Jack Corbin. Or any other man at the moment. "I know you'll find this hard to believe, but I am very, no, extremely, happy with things the way they are in my life. I've finally proved to myself I don't need a man to be complete.''

Clarice shot her an exaggeratedly appalled look over the rim of her sunglasses. ''Heresy.''

''No, if I ever start looking again, it'll be the flip side of J.D. The kind of man who drives a nice ordinary Buick or Chevrolet. A man with roots. Feet on the ground. Steady. Dependable.''

''Boorrring!''

Annie laughed. ''Boring can have its selling points.''

''Not if you're talking about men. You've got to be willing to get burned a time or two to ferret out a good one.''

''Then they ought to come with warning labels.''

Clarice laughed now. ''Oh, Annie, most of the time they do, we just choose to ignore them.''

NO DENYING IT. Jack was having his share of serious misgivings by the time he pulled into the C.M. parking lot just after five o'clock on Tuesday afternoon.

Who, of all the employees at this picnic, would be glad to see him coming? No one. He, after all, was the guy in the black cape, the one with *villain* scrawled across his back in big bold letters. Had he secretly hoped they might understand that everything ran its course, had its time? That the glory days of C.M. were over, and he was merely the one taking the steps to put it out of its misery.

No, he didn't expect them to understand that. Probably should never have said he'd come to the thing in the first place, but Annie had flung the invitation at him as a challenge. And he wasn't a man to ignore a challenge.

He parked his car at the back of the lot, got out, and reached in the back seat for the basket of fried chicken he and Essie had spent the past two hours making. He'd been more hindrance than help, he was sure, but Essie had been so thrilled to hear that he was attending the picnic, she had practically floated around the kitchen fixing his mistakes, two of which had included a dozen eggs splattered on the brick floor and a measuring cup of flour upended on the countertop.

The parking lot was full. The factory itself sat on twenty acres of what had once been prime farmland. Its owners had sold out and moved back to Ohio some twenty-five years ago. Jack's father had bought the property for its flatness and the fact that it was surrounded by Virginia mountains, the trees lit up every fall with colors only nature could blend. Now, in September, they hugged the level piece of land on which C.M. sat in an embrace of green.

Music floated out from behind the building. Bluegrass. It had been years since he'd heard the twangy notes of a fiddle. Homesickness knifed through him with an unexpected edge. The sound brought with it a deluge of memory, fiddler's conventions he'd gone to as a boy with his dad who had loved the folk music and taught Jack to appreciate it. Booths set up with candy apples and hot cakes, Jack's father letting him use his own money and his own judgment in buying the treats. Jack had always gone home with a stomachache. Joshua had believed in letting his son make his own mistakes, reasoning that was the only way he would remember them.

The factory itself was an enormous brick building, tall pane windows letting in plenty of natural light. Joshua Corbin had wanted to give his employees an appealing place to come to work every day. "Light affects a man's soul, son. We weren't made to live in the dark." The words echoed in Jack's head as if he'd just heard his father say them.

He followed the music, rounding the corner of the building. Hundreds of people filled the grass yard in front of him. Adults—young, old—teenagers and toddlers. What looked like the whole town. He wasn't sure what he'd expected, but not this. Laughter. Smiling faces. Some flat foot dancing up front by the bluegrass trio. On the stage hung a banner that read: C.M. THANK YOU FOR THE GOOD YEARS.

Jack blinked, surprised.

Fifty feet or so out from the music were tables of food. He looked down at the basket of chicken in his own hand and felt like an intruder at someone else's party.

But a round-faced woman with soft gray hair bustled up just then, taking the offering from him. "Come right on in. Um, this smells good. You make it yourself?"

"Had a little help," he said.

"What's your name, young man?"

"Jack," he said, feeling like the Grinch about to steal Christmas.

"I'm Ethel Myers. Retired now. Worked here for twenty years, though. Still miss it."

He could do little more than nod.

She waved him inside. "Go in and get comfortable now. We're just about ready to eat. Iced tea and lemonade set up on those tables over there."

"Thank you, ma'am."

"You're surely welcome," she said and waved a greeting to another latecomer.

Jack weaved his way through the crowd, recognizing some faces, sure he heard someone murmur his name. He picked up a glass of sweet tea from the table Ethel had directed him to, then stood there on the periphery of the crowd, wondering at the jovial tone of the gathering. His understanding from Annie had been that this was a farewell picnic of sorts for those who had worked at C.M. He'd fully expected to be the target of seriously grim head-shaking. Had maybe even brought himself here because on some level, he thought he deserved their ire for not giving the factory another chance.

There wasn't any to be found.

This felt more like a celebration. Balloons in a rainbow of colors bracketed the tables set up around him, all of which were loaded with so much food they practically groaned beneath the weight.

"Well, I'll be darned."

A man in bib overalls and a red plaid shirt stuck his hand out to Jack and said, "You're Joshua's boy, aren't you?"

Jack shook the man's hand and nodded. "Yes, sir, I am."

"Woulda known you anywhere. Look just like him."

The statement was made with a thread of surprise running through it, but mostly gladness, which startled Jack more than a little.

"I'm Henry Sigmon. Your daddy hired me, let's see, nineteen years ago, I guess. Company wasn't such a big thing then. But I needed a job, and he gave me one. Been here ever since. I remember him bringing you to the Christmas lunches. Sure was proud of you."

"Lot of good food at those lunches."

Henry gave a you-better-believe-it nod. "We've got some unbelievable cooks around here."

Jack managed a smile, the man's recollection stirring up an unexpected pang inside him. Even then, he had known his father was proud of him, and there wasn't anything else in Jack's life since then that had created that same sense of worthiness. Not a degree from Duke. Nor the career he'd made for himself.

"Wish this had ended up differently, you know?" Henry's smile had disappeared, in its place obvious disappointment. "For the last couple years, most of the people here have done what they could to lighten the load. Taking regular pay for overtime hours, closing down the day-care center your father built.''

''Day-care center?'' The question was out before Jack had time to wonder what the man would think about his not knowing such a thing.

Henry looked surprised but said, ''Yeah. Built about ten years ago, I guess. Sure did make a difference for a lot of families. Moms and dads could go spend their breaks and lunches with their children. Not having the expense of child care made working more realistic for a number of people. But no doubt it took a lot to keep it running, so everybody voted to close it six months ago since the company just seemed to keep losing money.''

Henry shook his head. ''Wish we could have pulled it out for you. Would have meant a lot to a good many of us. Being able to do that for your father. It would've been a nice way to pay him back for everything he did for us.''

Jack tried for a response, but the words stuck in his throat. Again all he could do was nod. None of what Henry Sigmon had just said should have made any difference to him. But it did somehow. He'd convinced himself there wasn't anything personal about the closing of this factory. He had a feeling he was going to be very, very wrong.

ANNIE SPOTTED HIM from the other side of the crowd.

It would have been impossible to miss him.

First of all, he was taller than nearly every other

man at the picnic. Second, he looked about as comfortable being here as a cat in the middle of a dog show.

Her first inclination—the one she would have followed last night while lamenting the fact that anyone could be heartless enough to just auction off this place—was to let him feel the pinch of that a while longer.

Her second—the one that could not deny that Jack Corbin didn't seem like a bad guy, just one misled—had her weaving her way through the crowd.

She tapped him on the shoulder. "You made it," she said.

He turned, looking relieved to see her. "Yeah. Even brought some chicken."

"No pancakes?"

A smile touched his too-appealing mouth.

She took pity on him. Couldn't help it. She'd invited him here, not sure what his welcome would be. He didn't strike her as a man to be cowed by much in life, but in his shoes, most people would have been.

"How about saying hello to a few people?"

"Sure," he said with a nod.

Annie led the way to a group a few yards away. She put a hand on Estelle Thompson's shoulder and said, "Estelle, this is Jack Corbin."

Estelle stepped back to allow the two of them entrance into the circle. "Well, I'd recognize you anywhere," Estelle said, beaming a smile at Jack. "I'm sure you don't remember me, but I started working here shortly after your daddy built on the new section.''

"Yes, ma'am," Jack said. "It's nice to see you."

For the next fifteen minutes, Annie introduced and re-introduced Jack to as many people as she could. Maybe she could make him see that real people with real families were going to be devastated by the closing of this factory.

Several dozen introductions later, Annie tipped her head toward the end of the field opposite the bluegrass band where Tommy and a group of boys were hurling baseballs at one another's gloves. "Say hi?"

Looking relieved, Jack nodded and followed her through the crowd of people. They stopped a few yards short of the boys' circle.

"Point taken," he said.

"Hope I didn't use too big a stick."

"Big enough."

Annie looked down, feeling more like a bully than she cared to. "For a lot of people, losing their job here will mean having to change their lives, Jack. Moving to another place."

Silence stretched out between them, more contemplative than awkward. Annie sensed he was considering her words, weighing them against his own conscience. And suddenly she felt hopeful again.

"Got a good arm on him," Jack said finally, nodding toward Tommy who had just thrown the ball to one of the other boys.

Annie folded her arms across her chest, hoping she

didn't sound like a mother hen when she said, "I almost wish he'd show no talent whatsoever for the sport."

"Why's that?"

"It's an awfully hard way to make a living."

"Aren't too many roads that make it easy."

"He's just so determined to be as good as his dad. But what if he's not? I don't want him to spend his life feeling like he didn't measure up." Annie pressed her lips together. She hardly knew this man. Why had she just told him that?

"You're his mother," he said, understanding in his voice. "That's natural. But the only way we ever figure those things out is to try."

Annie sighed. "And I've already figured out that the quickest way for me to encourage him is by discouraging him."

Jack stared off into the distance for a moment. "When I was growing up, there was this swimming hole in the creek behind our house. My mother's greatest fear was that I'd fall in and drown when no one was looking. It was the one thing she asked me not to do, but of course, every chance I got I had to sneak out there. I think Mother Nature just wires boys up to do the opposite of what their parents want them to do."

"As if the job needed any more hurdles," she said, shaking her head. And then, again realizing it was an awfully personal conversation for two people who didn't know one another to be having, she added,

"I'm sorry. I didn't mean to bore you with mother-worries."

He looked at her, and the moment stood still. "I wasn't bored."

"Hey, Mr. Corbin! Wanna play?" Tommy waved hard, baseball in hand, saying something to the little boy next to him.

"Do you mind?" Jack asked.

"Of course not," she said, clearing her throat and dropping her gaze.

Jack jogged over to the boys who immediately buzzed around him like little bees. A few of them, including Tommy, she was happy to see, offered the use of their gloves. "I'm probably running the risk of an injury hard as you boys are throwing, but let me try a few without first," Jack said.

The boys gave a round of serious nods, happy, Annie suspected, to at least be considered a threat. They backed out from one another to form a circle and began throwing the ball. Six years old and not a boy among them took the exercise as anything less than dead serious.

"I see Tommy stole him out from under our noses, hmm?"

Annie turned around. Clarice had a glass of lemonade in one hand, her sunglasses in the other. "Pancakes and baseball. Apparently works for both boys and men."

Clarice chuckled. "Heavens, he's fine."

Annie followed her sister's gaze, blatantly assessing as it was. It was hard to deny the declaration. He was wearing a blue short-sleeve shirt, the defined muscles of his shoulders standing out each time he threw the ball. "Down, girl."

Clarice gave a little shiver. "I told myself good looks shouldn't get in the way of objectivity. I'm the editor of the county newspaper. He's about to drain us dry of five hundred jobs. Don't let hormones get in the way of good common sense, Clarice, I told myself. Common sense be damned."

Annie smiled a stiff smile and refused even to consider the prick of envy her sister's assessment sent along her nerve endings.

For the next fifteen minutes, the two of them stood and watched. The game stopped for a minute when Jack went over to help one of the boys adjust his glove.

"Wonder why he's never married," Clarice said.

"Probably some reason you'd rather not know."

"Like?"

"Oh, I don't know. That he goes through women like water?"

"Says who?"

"If someone hasn't snagged him yet, he's probably not snaggable."

"The catch is all the more appealing for the challenge." A pause and then, "Maybe he's just never found the right person."

"Is that wistfulness I hear in your voice?"

"Just a tad, maybe."

They stood watching, silent for a while. Jack was generous with praise for the boys' efforts, each of them beaming with pride at being singled out, but none of them more so than Tommy. Like a plant someone had forgotten to water, Tommy positively blossomed under Jack's encouraging, ''Atta boy, Tommy! Awesome catch!''

Watching them, Annie felt a wearing sense of defeat. Since J.D. had left, she'd sensed Tommy's certainty that he must somehow be responsible for it. The very thought of that both enraged and saddened her beyond anything she could have imagined. What she'd wanted to give Tommy most was what she had not had in her own childhood. Stability, that grounding sense that all was right in his world.

''Know what you're thinking,'' Clarice said. ''Don't go there.''

''I feel like I'm depriving him of something he needs so much.''

''First,'' Clarice said, index finger popping up, ''you aren't the one depriving that child of anything. His father has taken care of that nicely, and any child would be lucky to have a mother so determined to make up for it. Annie, I've never known anyone to work harder at anything than you do at being a good mother. I know how important it is to you to give Tommy some of the things we didn't have growing up. And it would be nice if J.D. had turned out to be father of the year, but he isn't. That's a fact. That's not your fault. And it's not Tommy's.''

"You're right. It's just—"

"He's happy, Annie. Just believe that, okay?"

She wanted to. She really wanted to. Looking out at her son right now, she almost could.

CHAPTER FIVE

FROM THE CORNER of his eye, Jack saw Annie and her sister turn and head back across the field. He'd felt their gazes on him for the last little while, heard Clarice's laughter tinkle across the lawn, suspected they were talking about him, wondered what they were saying.

He spent another half hour with the group of boys. There were some pretty good arms among them for six-year-olds, Tommy's notably the best. Not something Annie would be thrilled to know, but it was true. He definitely had a knack for the game.

The group broke up, and Tommy followed him back across the field. "Did you ever collect baseball cards, Mr. Corbin?"

"Sure did. Had a great Hank Aaron."

"Really?"

"Yep. Still have it, I think," Jack said, remembering the box he'd kept all his cards in and making a mental note to look for it back at the house.

"Wow. That must be worth a lot. Where did you get it?"

"My dad bought it for me."

"My dad said he's going to get me some good

ones, but he keeps forgetting. I bet next time I see him he'll have them.''

''Bet he will,'' Jack agreed. So that explained the concern in Annie's eyes when Tommy had talked about his dad last night at dinner. Jack had never made fatherhood a priority in his life, but he couldn't begin to understand having a little boy who spoke of him with adoration hanging off every word and not being downright grateful for it.

''I need to go to the little boys' room,'' Tommy said.

''Want me to find your mom?'' Jack asked.

''I can go myself. It's over there.''

''Okay.'' At the men's room door, Jack said, ''I'll wait right here.''

'''Kay,'' Tommy said and darted inside.

Jack nodded at a couple of men standing a few yards away. One of them pulled a pack of Redman tobacco from his back pocket, ferreted out a good-size pinch and stuck it in his mouth.

''Damn shame to see all this go down the toilet,'' the tobacco-less one said.

The one with his mouth full nodded, positioned the chew at the back corner of his jaw. ''Actually thought that Annie McCabe might be able to do something about it. Turns out she's not much of a mayor. Just like her husband, I guess.''

''Ex,'' the other one said.

''Yeah. Town shoulda held a new election altogether after he ran off. There's gotta be somebody around here more qualified than a pampered jock's wife. She's probably real good at setting up nail appointments, but what the heck does that have to do with running a town?''

The other man shrugged. ''From everything I've read in the newspaper, she's been the only one trying to get that Jack Corbin not to sell out.''

The man made a noise that sounded like disbelief. Either that, or he was choking. ''Well, her sister's the editor, so how much of that can you believe?''

Tommy bounded out of the bathroom. ''I'm really hungry, Mr. Corbin.''

Jack looked down at the little boy. ''Then let's go get some food.''

They headed back across the grass lawn to the dozen or so tables loaded with homemade offerings. No sign that the boy had overheard those men, but even so an urge to protect him sprang up from some unidentifiable place.

So was that what everyone here thought? That Annie was a joke as mayor? Were they judging her by the fact that she hadn't managed to save Corbin Manufacturing? That seemed a few miles short of fair to him. But people were going to think what they wanted. And if they were aiming darts at anyone, it ought to be at him.

Why then did he feel so bad about Annie being their target instead?

"NOW ANNIE, I just don't know how I feel about setting up that dunking booth this year if you're going to be the one getting plastered. I have to say we've got some folks with pretty good aim around here."

"Reverend Landers, if it's part of the mayor's job to sit in the dunking booth for the Lord's Acre Sale, then I have no intention of changing tradition."

"Well, J.D. wasn't real keen on the idea when we discussed it. I mean back before he—"

"I'll be happy to do it, Reverend Landers," Annie insisted, trying to head off that particular line of conversation.

"Well, if you're sure."

She glanced over at the field where the boys had made a prisoner of Jack. They were no longer there. "I need to go find my son. You go right ahead and reserve that booth."

The reverend nodded. "All right, Annie. But it'll be a really bad hair day."

Annie laughed. If only that were the worst of her problems. One circle around the perimeter of the crowd, and she found Tommy sitting beside Jack at a picnic table, a plate in front of him that actually included a helping of broccoli and two carrots.

At the sight of her, Jack stood and said, "Hope it was all right for Tommy to eat."

"Sure," Annie said.

"Hi, Mama." Tommy picked up a carrot and stuck it in his mouth. "Mr. Corbin said people who play baseball or any other kind of sport need to make their bodies strong by eating stuff that's good for them. It's like fuel we put in cars only it tastes better.''

"Some powers of persuasion, Jack," Annie said.

A smile hit his mouth, raising an instant alert sign inside her. "Been told so once or twice."

A more confident woman, Clarice, surely, might have called that response flirtatious. Might have acted on it. Sent him one right back with the same kind of edge to it. But Annie's confidence with the opposite sex had gone west with J.D. and his twenty-something blonde.

"Thank you for helping Tommy with his plate," she said, not quite meeting his gaze. "Aren't you having anything? There's plenty of good food."

"I'm okay right now."

"Hey, Annie."

She glanced around to find Tim Filmore aiming one of his I'm-so-sexy smiles at her. He was tall and skinny, the legs exposed beneath khaki safari shorts looking like number two pencils in hiking boots. Convinced he'd been put on earth for the explicit purpose of wowing the fairer sex, he had coal-black hair that looked as though it had been steam-ironed, then glued into place with a good three ounces of mousse for insurance. Cologne hung around him like early-morning fog in San Francisco.

Annie sneezed and with no graceful exit in sight, said, "Tim, this is Jack Corbin. Jack, Tim works with Clarice at the newspaper."

"Lead reporter," Tim said, pumping the hand Jack

stuck out like the handle on the pump of a well long gone dry.

"Nice to meet you," Jack said, rubbing an eye no doubt as offended as Annie's nose.

"So you're the man bringing all this to an end," Tim said, puffing his chest out and cocking his chin. He reminded Annie of a banty rooster confronting another rooster of a much bigger breed, strutting across the chicken yard with fists raised.

To his credit, Jack looked anything but intimidated. And if Tim hadn't long since fine-tuned Annie's dislike of him, she might have actually felt sorry for him. It was as if Mother Nature, having shortchanged him on the outward ability to attract the opposite sex, had loaded him up with an extra dose or two of testosterone so that confidence was never going to be a problem for him.

"In a manner of speaking," Jack said, the words as smooth as steel and with just as hard an edge.

"Quote you on that?" Tim threw out.

Annie felt like a bystander watching a wreck about to happen. The question: should she throw herself out in front of the oncoming cars or simply pray they swerved in time?

"Yes, as a matter of fact. And add this to it: I am solely responsible for the decision to shut down Corbin Manufacturing. And despite the mayor's very admirable efforts on this town's behalf, this company was ruined a long time before it was handed over to me. As far as I can tell, it'd be impossible to fix a cannonball gash with a Band-Aid. If you'll excuse me, Annie. Nice to meet you, Tim. See ya later, Tommy.''

"Bye, Mr. Corbin."

"You, too, Jack," Tim threw out, a swagger in his voice. Clearly, he considered Jack the one to swerve at the last second. "He's got some nerve, coming here like he belongs—"

"He owns the place, Tim," Annie said. "What part of that makes you think he doesn't belong here?"

"The part that says he's a traitor?"

"You know, Tim, you might want to tone down the hostility just a shade or two. It's not exactly a win-over technique.''

"I'm not so sure about that. Maybe that's why you haven't gotten anywhere with him."

Annie counted to ten. And then back to one.

"Maybe if the two of us put our heads together, we could come up with the right game plan."

"Thanks, Tim. I wouldn't want to steal your glory,''

"I'm a generous kind of guy. There are a lot of things I'd be willing to share with you, Annie."

Forever. She was staying single forever. "Tommy, let's go take a look at the dessert table," she said, ignoring the statement and its implications. "I'm feeling the need for something with chocolate in it. Something really big with chocolate in it."

"All right!" Tommy said, leaping up to grab Annie's hand and tug her along behind him. Of course he already knew where to find it.

JACK LEFT THE CROWD and headed inside the building, putting some much-needed distance between himself and that Filmore guy. He'd all but undressed Annie with his beady eyes. And he didn't know which had been more offensive, the man's cologne or his outrageous flirting.

But then hadn't Jack been flirting with her himself right before Filmore came up?

He took a detour around his own question, finding himself standing in the doorway of his father's old office. He stepped inside and closed the door. Surrounded by Joshua's things, all of which Jack was surprised to see were still as they'd been the last time he had been in here, a strange kind of comfort settled around him, as if some piece of his father were still here.

He crossed the wood floor and sat down in the leather chair behind the big cherry desk. Pictures took up most of the space. One of his mother. An eight-by-ten in a gold frame. She was young. Little more than a teenager. It must have been taken before they'd married. She'd been beautiful in the classic sense. High cheekbones, full lips, straight dark hair.

Next to her photo was a collection of smaller frames capturing Jack in different phases of boyhood. One when he was about three showed him on the back of a Percheron—Sam's mother, he thought. Jack's father stood at the side, a proud smile on his face.

Another, at seven or eight, pictured him in his little-league football uniform, his stick arms making a mockery of his muscle-man pose. A junior high class photo. Graduation shot.

"Hello, Jack."

Jack turned from the window. A man with gray hair and an uncertain smile stood at the office entrance.

"How are you?" The man stepped forward and stuck out his hand.

Jack recognized him then. "Hugh. Good, and you?" He had last seen Hugh Kroner, C.M.'s vice president, at his father's funeral. He appeared to have aged a couple of decades since then. His eyes were red-rimmed with bags beneath, and his face had deep grooves carved in it.

"Pretty good. Wish you had a more pleasant reason for being here."

"So do I."

Hugh glanced at the desktop. "Anything I can help you do?"

Jack shook his head. "But I appreciate the offer."

"It's too bad things didn't turn out differently."

"It was a solid company for a long time."

"Everything runs its course, I guess," Hugh said. "It's just hard to see a place close its doors when it's been around as long as this company has."

Jack nodded.

Hugh sent another glance across the desk, then

nodded toward the window. "Well, better get back out there. If there's anything I can do, Jack. Anything at all."

"Thanks, Hugh."

Jack went to the window, watching the older man weave his way back into the crowd of people still eating hamburgers and hot dogs. Had the demise of this company hung all those years on Hugh?

This afternoon had not turned out at all as he'd expected. Where he'd been prepared for hostility, he'd gotten friendliness. Where he'd expected resentment, he'd gotten gratitude for the opportunity to have had what was for years a good company to come to work for every day.

Those people out there were celebrating the end of what had once been something really good and valuable to them. So many of the ailing businesses he'd gotten inside over the past eight years had not only been crippled by some near-fatal blow, but also suffered the equally stunning trauma of a workforce that turned against it and who considered the company itself somehow to blame for its fate and theirs as well.

This was apparently untrue at C.M. It made Jack feel grateful and a little humbled.

"A business has to make money to exist, son. But in addition to that, one of my greatest responsibilities is to make it the kind of place where people look forward to coming each day." Jack glanced out the window at the group of people who were thoroughly enjoying themselves. It looked as if his father had done what he'd set out to do.

For so many years, Jack had focused on how much his father had disappointed him. A sharp pain knifed through his chest, at its tip a piercing sense of regret for the fact that he was about to let this company be auctioned off like some dead, worthless thing.

And yet his own wounded pride hadn't let him consider doing anything else.

He thought about all the people he'd met earlier, of how many of them were about to lose jobs they'd had for twenty-five years, and yet not one of them had been anything other than polite and respectful to him. In finding a new way to make a living, none of them would be able to afford the luxury of pride.

There in a moment of clarity, Jack's reasons for selling off the company seemed the height of pettiness. And suddenly, he wasn't too sure he liked the man he must appear to be.

ANNIE SETTLED IN AT her desk the next morning with a cup of coffee, which she used to wash down the aspirin serving as her breakfast.

She had left the picnic without seeing Jack again, then donated another night of sleep to agonizing over her increasingly desperate hope that he would reconsider the dead-end road along which he planned to send Corbin Manufacturing.

She picked up the phone and dialed into her voice mail. "You have two new messages."

The first was a hang-up. The second made her set down her coffee cup with a thump.

"Annie, this is Jack. Call me at the factory when you get in this morning." And he left a number that would ring direct to him.

Annie clicked off and punched the number in as quickly as her fingers could follow the demand from her sleep-addled brain. *Don't get your hopes up, Annie.* Chances are nothing has changed. But for this town, she couldn't help but hope differently. Hope that Jack might have been affected by the people he'd met yesterday and the direness of what was about to happen to their livelihoods. Hope he had seen them as individuals who needed his company to make ends meet.

Jack answered with a distracted-sounding hello.

"It's Annie. I just got your message."

"I've postponed the auction."

"You—what?" Annie's voice came out several notes higher than its normal range. She cleared her throat. "I mean, really—"

"No promises, Annie," he said quickly, quietly. "I just want to make sure I've made the right decision. It seems like the responsible thing to do."

"Yes, well," Annie began, not sure what to make of this. He had postponed the auction, not called it off. But postponing was a start at least. "Thank you, Jack. I have to say I really hope you'll see something that will make you change your mind."

"I know," he said, and here his voice changed notes. Was that regret she heard? "I'll be in touch."

Annie sat there with the phone in her hand until a recording came on and asked her to please hang up and try her party again.

She punched the off button and dropped the cordless onto her desk. Okay. So something must have happened at the picnic yesterday. Something significant enough to get him to take a closer look. At least they were moving in the right direction. *Patience then, Annie.* A change of heart was a change of heart. Whether it happened in one giant leap or a hundred baby steps. She didn't care.

ON FRIDAY AFTERNOON, Annie left work a little earlier than usual, resolving to leave her mayor's hat at the office. For tonight, she was simply a mother hosting a sleepover for her son and five of his friends.

At Macon's Point Elementary, Annie got in line and waited her turn around the circle where the children were picked up. The school had been built in the late forties, a two-story brick building with tall white pane windows. Boxwoods curved around the sides, more than a half century old. The building had the old-fashioned charm not found in many modern structures, and Annie loved it.

She spotted Tommy sixth or seventh back from the front and, as usual, her heart ka-thumped its gladness. It had taken a while for her to get used to him being in school every day. She'd missed him so much the first couple of months that she would drive out at recess time just to look at him on the playground. Of course, she never let him know this. He'd gotten a very early case of "I'm-not-a-baby-anymore-Mama," so she tried hard not to dote on him.

He climbed in the Tahoe now with a grin on his face just about half as wide as he was tall.

Annie smiled at him. "Excited?"

Tommy nodded. "Did you get the stuff?"

She reached over, gave him a kiss on the head. "Yep. Bought Patterson's out of every cap gun and feather headdress they had."

"All right!" Tommy shot a fist in the air.

Annie grinned. She couldn't help it. Her child's happiness was to her a gift in itself. She'd always felt the need to be careful of spoiling him. He was an only child; it would have been easy to do. But so far she'd seen no evidence of that, his joy at some of life's simple good things still pure in the way she remembered feeling as a little girl. And yes, she couldn't deny her own sense of needing to make up for the hurt J.D. had caused him.

She braked at the end of the circle, waved a couple of school buses past, then pulled out onto Hickory Street and handed Tommy a carton of his favorite fruit juice.

"Thanks, Mama," he said and took a long gulp. "Will Aunt Clarice be there tonight?"

"Later," Annie said. "She called this afternoon

and said she had to run up to Lexington to cover a story.''

Tommy nodded. ''Do you think it'll be there when we get home?''

''What's that, doodlebug?''

''My present from Daddy.''

Annie's grip tightened on the wheel. ''I don't know. Maybe.''

''I bet it will,'' Tommy said, hope in his voice. ''What do you think it'll be?''

''A new glove maybe?'' Annie played the game while pure fury churned inside her. Tommy had checked the mailbox every afternoon for the past week. Nothing J.D. had ever done—and he'd done a lot of things during their marriage—had infuriated her the way his cavalier treatment of their son's feelings did. She was long past over his betrayal of her, had planted a GOOD RIDDANCE! sign in her heart's front yard and was even glad now to be on her own. It had taken some time to admit it, but she'd spent most of her marriage to J.D. weighed down by the feeling that he was just waiting for something better to come along. She would do until then.

Something better had—at least in his eyes. And she was over that. Really, she was. But at moments like this, when she could hear the hurt in her son's voice, see it in the visible struggle on his face, she wished for the power—even if it was just for one day—to make J.D. feel the same kind of pain he was causing their son.

CHAPTER SIX

HE SHOULD HAVE CALLED first. What if she wasn't
home? What if she had company? A date?

*This was a bad idea, Jack. One of your recent
worst.*

True, he was anxious to talk to her. True, he did
have something for Tommy.

But, both could be accomplished later after he'd
called first.

Just as he was negotiating a U-turn, the sign for
her road popped up on the left. Apple Tree Lane. Just
as Essie had described in the directions she'd given
him a short while ago.

So he was here. Might as well see if she was at
home.

Jack wasn't sure what kind of house he'd expected
Annie to live in, but it wasn't the one he found at the
end of the gravel road deep in the heart of Langor
County. He'd had her figured for a city girl, and yet
the big white farmhouse said differently. The house
was old, the kind with character that couldn't be built
into a new house. Green shutters bracketed the windows. Flower boxes beneath each one held profusions
of red geraniums, refusing to give in to fall. A porch

ran the width of the house, terra-cotta flowerpots holding what looked like a collection of cooking herbs.

Jack followed the circular driveway and parked his car beneath a tall old maple tree. He got out, his feet leading him up the flagstone sidewalk to the front door where he stopped in mid-knock. Sounded like somebody was having a party in there. He threw a glance back at the driveway. Annie's car was the only other one here.

His knock was tentative. When no one came he knocked again. Footsteps sounded from inside, hurried, thwap, thwap, thwap, and then the door flew open.

And there stood Annie McCabe in full Indian war dress, pink, yellow and red feather headband, paint slashes on each cheek, a doe-colored leather dress with beading down the front. Looking just a shade chagrined.

"It's Tommy's rule," she said. "If you come to his birthday party, you have to dress up."

"Good one," he said, pointing at her costume.

"I passed muster, anyway."

Jack took a step back. "Look, I just stopped by to ask you a few questions. I'll call in the morning. Tomorrow."

"Oh, no," she said, taking him by the arm and tugging him through the front door. "That's the other rule. Once you're here, you have to stay. Wait. Don't go anywhere."

Jack did as he was told while Annie disappeared in the direction of what sounded like a giant cowboy and Indian battle. Whoops and hollers echoed out from the back of the house, the seriousness of the injuries denounced by a leavening dose of giggles.

The house smelled of just-baked cookies, fresh lemons. The foyer gave indication of its personality: a long wooden table sat against one wall, a walnut hutch against another. An old oil painting hung on the staircase wall.

Annie was back, carrying two things: a ten-gallon hat just about the size of the sofa in the living room behind her. And a fake handlebar mustache.

She held them both out to him and said, "These should fit."

Jack laughed, surprising himself. The past few days hadn't given him much to laugh about. He took the offerings, lowered the hat on his head like a crane placing a house in a new location and stuck the mustache on his upper lip.

This time it was Annie who laughed, a good long laugh that rose up from somewhere deep and left tears streaming through her war paint.

"You look…" she broke off, again overcome. Finally, touching a hand to her side, she said, "Like Hoss Cartwright."

"With a fake mustache."

She nodded, pressed her lips together. But still, her eyes danced. And he found himself glad that he'd been the one to put that look there.

"Come on," she said and tipped her head toward the battle being waged somewhere in the direction of her backyard.

They followed a hallway that led through what was obviously a family room. He had a quick impression of a couple of comfortable-looking leather couches, framed photos of Tommy from a baby onward atop a round mahogany table. They stepped through a set of French doors into a huge yard enclosed with a white picket fence. Here the cowboys and Indians, six or seven boys altogether, were waging the battle he'd heard from the foyer. At the sidelines stood an enormous dog, chocolate-cake Cyrus, no doubt, who had been decked out in a Pony Express costume, leather saddlebags hanging from either side.

"Mr. Corbin!" Tommy spotted them and came running across the yard. His spurs jangled behind pointy-toed cowboy boots, and from the holster at his side hung a neon-green plastic water gun.

"Looks like it's been a wet battle," Jack said.

Tommy grinned, and Jack saw on his face happiness, pure and real. "Isn't this a great party?"

"About the best I've ever seen. Your mom do all this?"

Tommy nodded. "She's pretty cool, huh?"

"I'll say," Jack said, glancing at Annie who looked pleased by her son's compliment.

"Whose team do you wanna be on, Mr. Corbin?"

"Call me Jack, and how about I take turns to keep it fair?"

"Okay!" Tommy grabbed his hand and tugged him into the fray. "But either way, you're gonna get wet!"

WATCHING FROM THE sidelines, something deep inside Annie ached for the fact that Tommy's own father would never in a million years have been out there in the middle of what to this group of boys was heaven on earth.

How had she managed to pick a man as a husband who couldn't get past entertaining himself long enough to even think about entertaining a child?

It was a question she'd asked herself many times, and the main foundation of her own lack of confidence in her ability to choose more wisely next time. What guarantee was there that she would do better?

Jack, drenched to the skin, was now taking a relieved-looking Cyrus's place as pack horse, one boy on his back, Tommy on his shoulders. When they squeezed with their legs, he responded with an appropriate gait, his tall hat bumping Tommy in the nose when he broke into a gallop, sending all the boys into a fit of giggles.

This went on for fifteen or twenty minutes until Jack finally collapsed onto the grass and declared exhaustion. Leaving them there, Annie slipped into the house and pulled Tommy's new cake from its hiding place. She positioned seven candles around its perimeter, set it in the middle of the kitchen table, then stuck her head out the door off the back of the kitchen. "Everybody, come on so we can sing 'Happy Birthday,' and Tommy can make his wish."

They came in a thunder of footsteps, crowding around the table and offering up exclamations of delight for the three-tiered cake before them.

Lagging behind was Jack, still wearing his hat and a now limp mustache. He met her gaze, smiled, and held the look for just a second too long to be deemed casual, long enough to knock her pulse up a beat or two.

And there was something on his face, Annie couldn't quite decide what it was, but something at least akin to contentment. The notion that this visit to her house had brought about that look was somehow pleasing to her. Lit a spot deep inside her that had once known how to be a woman in a man's presence. Oh, she wasn't kidding herself…he'd been outside roughhousing with a herd of very exuberant boys, a hero in their midst. Still…

She chopped the thought off right there, whirled around and got busy lighting Tommy's candles, giving herself a good scolding in the process. *What in the world are you thinking, Annie McCabe?* Talk about jumping from the pan into the fire! So maybe J.D. wouldn't have thrown himself out in the middle of those boys, but as far as Annie could tell, Jack lived his life with a great big GLAD TO BE SINGLE sign on his back. And that was fine. Nothing wrong with it. Especially when a man was up-front about it. Which J.D. had not been.

She'd realized at some point along the journey to divorce that he had never really wanted to be married. She'd been a convenience. Like the Mini-Mart just around the corner where you could dash in when you ran out of eggs. Someone to keep his clothes washed, his meals on the table...and the worst part? She'd let him treat her that way! Doormat Annie.

"That's some cake," Jack said, interrupting her silent lecture. "Did you make it?"

Annie turned, met his complimentary gaze and nodded. "Actually, twice. Once for Cyrus. And another for Tommy."

Jack smiled. "I can see why he couldn't resist. How do you find time to be such a good mother and mayor of Macon's Point?"

The compliment startled Annie, and then sent a trickle of warmth down her center. "I love my son. Doing things for him isn't work. It's a part of my life I wouldn't trade for anything."

"He's a lucky boy."

Annie dipped her chin, brushed a nonexistent speck from her dress. "Thank you."

"Mama, can I blow them out now? I know what my wish is!" Tommy had taken the chair at the head of the table and was itching to get on with the tradition.

"Sure. Let's light them up." Annie pulled a pack of matches from the pocket of her dress.

"Want me to do that?" Jack offered.

"Okay, just don't catch your mustache on fire," she said.

They both laughed then, and the moment had a familiarity to it that defied explanation. Undeniable, though, this tug of attraction low inside her. *No, Annie.* Not this one. Not this time.

One of the boys started the happy birthday song, and they all joined in, Jack surprising her with a very on-key rendition. When they'd finished, she grabbed her camera from the kitchen counter, positioned herself at the other end of the table. "Okay, ready, set."

Tommy drew in a big gulp of air, fanned out the candle flames on top of his cake in a single blow. Everyone cheered.

"Presents or cake first?" Annie asked Tommy.

"Presents!" he said. All the other boys clapped their agreement.

Annie looked at Jack. "As if I needed to ask that question."

She handed Tommy the first one, and he tore into it with the excitement of having waited three hundred sixty-five days for this moment. And Annie was proud to say that he showed equal enthusiasm and appreciation for each of the gifts from his friends, giving them all a "Wow! Thank you!" that made her beam a little inside. It was a lesson she had tried hard to teach him, the meaning of a gift, and that in addition to the present itself, it meant that another person had taken the time to pick out something they thought would be special to him.

"He's a good boy, Annie," Jack said in a low voice by her side. "You must be really proud of him."

"I am," she said. And even though he had no way of knowing it, there wasn't a compliment in the world that would have meant more to Annie.

Tommy had opened the last of his gifts. "Boy, was that great!" he said.

"That's a lot of good stuff," Annie said.

Jack dipped his head close to Annie. "I have a little something for Tommy. Kind of a coincidence, but do you mind if I give it to him now?"

"Of course not," she said, surprised.

Jack reached in his back pocket for his wallet. He opened it, pulled something out, then stepped forward and handed it to Tommy. "I did a little digging around the attic and found this. I'd like for you to have it."

Tommy took it, stared at it for several seconds, his eyes wide. "It's your Hank Aaron card."

"Yep. It's yours."

"Wow. Thanks, Jack!"

"You're welcome."

"Jack, that's an unbelievable gift," Annie said, not sure what to say.

"When I was a boy, I thought so, too. And I had a pretty good idea it would mean as much to Tommy now as it did to me then."

Annie swallowed, but a lump of sorts had settled in her throat and made her eyes water. "Thank you," she said again, and then busied herself with cutting the cake and getting each of the boys a slice. All the while thinking about the look on Tommy's face when they'd gotten home that afternoon, and the mailman had failed yet again to deliver a birthday present from his father.

"THAT'S THE BEST CAKE I've ever eaten in my life," Jack said, and not a single word of it was flattery. It really was. Each layer had been topped with what looked like an inch of cream-cheese icing, every bite melting in his mouth. "Did you go to cooking school or something, Annie?"

She laughed, flattered in spite of the common sense flag that had all but folded itself up at his words. "Self-taught."

Jack shook his head and aimed his fork at another bite. "Unbelievable."

The doorbell rang. "I promise we're going to get around to the reason you came over in the first place," she said. "Let me just go get this."

"I'm not exactly suffering," he said. Most of the women he knew were on a first-name basis with Sara Lee as in frozen goods, not Betty Crocker as in cookbooks. He stretched for one last glimpse before she disappeared down the hallway, a poof of physical attraction going off inside him. *Don't go there, Jack.*

The kind of woman he normally dated had no interest in home and hearth. That was deliberate on his part. He liked women who had their own plans for the future, and they didn't include settling down and turning in their laptops for aprons. It was just a lot less complicated when both parties expected the same thing going in.

Jack had long ago decided he wasn't the marrying type. Life worked just fine without it. A man who lived the way he lived had no need for permanence of any sort.

So what are you doing in Annie's kitchen thinking what a great chocolate cake she makes and how good she looks in that dress?

"Jack! What a nice surprise!"

Annie's sister, Clarice, led the way back into the kitchen. He caught her curious expression and said, "I'm afraid I interrupted Tommy's birthday party."

"Nice hat," she said, her smile dimming a little.

He gave the top a pat. "You missed the mustache. Sacrificed it for the chocolate cake."

Behind Clarice, Annie laughed. "You should have seen him, Clar. He could have been on Bonanza."

"It was image-changing, all right," Jack agreed, catching Annie's eye.

Annie glanced away, quickly.

Jack looked at Clarice who was clearly assessing what had just passed between the two of them. She wasn't smiling.

His own smile faded. Why, he wasn't sure. But he found himself saying, "I had some questions for Annie about C.M. We were just about to get around to that."

"Oh," Clarice said. "Sorry to interrupt."

"Clarice, you aren't interrupting anything," Annie said. "How about a piece of Tommy's cake?"

"No, thanks. I just wanted to drop by, see how his party went. Give him a hug for me, okay? I've gotta go. I really need to get this story over to the paper. Last-minute addition."

"But you just got here," Annie said.

"I know, but I really shouldn't have stopped in the first place. Nose to the grindstone. I'll talk to you tomorrow, okay?"

She waved at them both, then headed back down the hall. Jack heard the front door open, then close.

"I'm sorry," Annie said, looking at him. "I think she just had a really long day."

Jack got up, put his fork and plate in the sink. He wasn't exactly sure what had just happened here, but Clarice's disapproval still hung in the air like newly sprayed air freshener. He felt, suddenly, that he should go. "You know, our talk can wait until tomorrow. Do you think you could come out to the factory around eleven?"

"Sure," she said, "but we can talk now. I'm sorry all the rest of this kept us from—"

"All the rest was great. Really great. But tomorrow will be just fine," he said, needing, with increasing urgency, to be on his way. He meant what he'd just said, but there was something about this house, this woman, that made him want to stay. Which meant he had to go. The sooner the better.

LATER, LYING IN BED, sleep was the last thing on Annie's mind. Too many questions scuffling for position in her thoughts.

What horrible punishment could she think up for J.D. without setting foot in California?

Why had Jack come over in the first place tonight?

And why had Clarice bolted off as though she'd just seen a ghost?

The first she'd have to think on. The next she couldn't answer. The third she could settle with a phone call. Annie had never been able to sleep when there was something wrong between Clarice and her. This time was no different. Two rings, and a groggy hello.

"Were you asleep?" Annie asked.

"You know good and well I wasn't."

"Well, I figured, so why'd you leave like that?"

Silence and then, "I thought you said you weren't interested in him!"

"You mean Jack?"

"Well, who else?" Hurt indignation muffled the question.

"I'm not!" Annie said. "Clarice, he came over to talk about the factory. He didn't know I was having a party for Tommy."

A pause and then, "Annie, I saw the look he gave you."

"What look?"

"The one that said he'd like to eat you up."

"Oh, Clarice," Annie said, certain now her sister

was being ridiculous. Men didn't look at her that way. Certainly not men like Jack Corbin. They looked at Clarice that way. "I don't know what you think you saw, but it wasn't that."

"Well, he certainly seemed to be having a good time," Clarice said, tone still in the hurt category, but leaning toward ready and willing to be convinced she was wrong.

"He enjoyed roughhousing with all those boys. And he brought Tommy a Hank Aaron baseball card for his birthday."

"Did he really?" Clarice asked, obviously impressed. "I bet Tommy loved that."

"He did," Annie said. She started to tell Clarice that J.D. hadn't bothered to get a present in the mail to his son, but she didn't want to add any fuel to her sister's overactive imagination by implying Jack's gift might have somehow lessened the hurt of that. "I'm not a factor. If you're interested in Jack, go for it."

"Are you sure?"

"Absolutely," she said, her assurance convincing to her own ears except for the pang of disappointment clutching her stomach.

By the time they hung up, all the tension of earlier had disappeared. Annie felt relieved as she always did to fix whatever might be off-kilter between the two of them. It was a role she was comfortable with. She'd always been the peacemaker even when she wasn't certain of their conflict.

Like tonight.

Obviously, Clarice thought she'd seen something that hadn't been there. And it really wasn't like her sister to be insecure where men were concerned. With good reason. A bat of the lashes was usually all it took to hook one. And Clarice had hooked more than her share. She'd just never found one who held her interest long enough that she wanted to keep him.

Annie had a feeling Jack might prove to be the exception.

And if that turned out to be the case, it was fine. Really.

She wasn't going to deny that she'd enjoyed his company tonight. Was grateful for his kindness to Tommy. And yes, he was an attractive man. Okay, very attractive.

He'd liked her chocolate cake. She'd give Clarice that much. But that wasn't exactly what made sparks fly between a man and a woman. Clarice was far better set up to accommodate that than Annie.

She refluffed her pillow, flopped over on her side. And missed, suddenly, having a man in her bed. She didn't miss J.D. Any feelings of that sort had climbed in the back seat of his convertible and ridden right on out of town with him.

But she did miss companionship. In the general sense of the word.

So why was she thinking about this now?

Here in the dark it was hard to deny the reason. She could deny it to Clarice all day long, but with the lights out, truth had a way of glowing so it was difficult to miss.

She flopped over again and gave her pillow another punch. Well, what red-blooded woman wouldn't get a little stirred up when a man like Jack walked in the room?

His appeal didn't need a lot of interpretation. But it had been a very long time since a man had affected Annie that way, good-looking or not. So maybe she should be glad of it. Happy to discover J.D. hadn't managed to deaden every nerve ending with his rejection of her and their family.

For a long time, that was exactly what she'd thought he had done. For months after he'd left Macon's Point, Annie had walked around feeling as if she'd been pumped full of Novocain. She could pinch herself and feel nothing.

Maybe part of it had been the realization that J.D. had turned into someone completely different from the man she'd married. Born with the kind of good looks and talent that seem like an unfair combination for one person to receive, he'd always had more than his share of confidence. And when he'd turned his attention on eighteen-year-old-greener-than-grass Annie, she'd been powerless to resist.

But when he'd started playing professional ball, he'd begun to change, seeing Annie as a roadblock to the extras that came with success. Women. Parties. She was the ball and chain tied to his ankle.

J.D.'s career-ending shoulder injury had come at a

time when she'd been ready to leave him. She had thought their move to Macon's Point and the change in lifestyle would save their marriage.

She'd been wrong.

She'd wallowed in the pain of that until one day she'd finally realized that she didn't want to spend the rest of her life trying to turn J.D. into something he wasn't. And so, with a new resolution—yes, I do want to have a life again—she had told herself that more than likely someone would come along, a man who might make her pulse leap, fill her stomach with butterflies. Only this time, she would be leading the charge with sharply-honed common sense and a fine-tuned checklist of husband/father character traits.

And so the numbness had finally faded into feeling again.

The next time she let someone into her life, she'd make sure they were on the same page about what they each considered important. For Annie, that was roots, belonging, being needed.

Clearly, Jack's life was anything but rooted. So even if Clarice hadn't set her sights on him, Jack wasn't the kind of man Annie would be looking for when she started looking.

And if Clarice wanted him, that was fine by her. She wanted her sister to be happy. Goodness knows she'd spent the better part of the last year helping Annie put her life back together.

Mistaken impression or not, Annie would make sure Clarice didn't see her as being in the way. If

Clarice thought Jack might be the one, then that was exactly what Annie wanted for her.

They were sisters, after all, and sisters always put each other first.

CHAPTER SEVEN

NINE MILES AWAY, Clarice hung up the phone, slid the slipping strap of her skimpy negligee back onto her shoulder and yanked the comforter all the way up to her neck. One day she was going to buy pajamas. The flannel kind like Annie wore when it was cold. One day. Clarice had always believed a woman should look like a woman in the bedroom. Which she did, pretty much without question. The only problem was there was no one here to tell her so. Or to appreciate it.

She was tired of being alone. Really tired.

She picked up the remote from the nightstand by the bed, zapped on the TV. Home Shopping Network. Another onion slicer for sale. This one was the best ever made, though. Slices in seconds. No mess, no fuss.

She flipped forward. MTV. What was he wearing?

Old reruns of *Magnum P.I.* Now, there was a man. That Tom Selleck… She put down the remote, smiled while Higgins gave the contrite-looking detective yet another lecture.

Clarice rolled over on her side, scuffled with her 310-count cotton sheets again. A commercial wiped

Magnum from the screen, the announcer's voice blaring into the room as if intent on getting his message across before the viewer had time to slap the mute button. Which she now did. And welcomed the silence. Oh, forget it, she just needed to get to sleep altogether. She flipped the TV off and lay there in the dark, waiting for sleepiness to hit her.

But she was wide awake, and the target of her thoughts was the conversation she'd just had with her sister. Questions kept aiming themselves like darts with the bull's-eye being: Was Jack interested in Annie?

He didn't seem like the domestic type. Annie defined domestic. Put Clarice to shame with her cooking. Annie was a born homemaker, had always wanted a real home. She needed a man now who could appreciate those good qualities in her. Someone unlike J.D. who never had. There were plenty of men out there who wanted the same things Annie wanted. But Clarice didn't think Jack was one of them.

There was no sibling rivalry involved here, was there? They were too old for that. Clarice loved her sister. Wanted nothing but the best for her. And if the right man for Annie came along, she'd be the first to step out of the way.

EARLY GUNTER HAD BEEN the security guard at the entrance of Corbin Manufacturing for at least a couple of decades. He waved when Annie pulled up to the gate just before eleven on Saturday morning.

Annie lowered her window. "Hey, Early."

Early was short with narrow shoulders and even less prominent hips. Despite the slight build, what was there was lean and muscled, strong like a locust fence post. He and his family went to the same church as Annie, and his wife was known as one of the best cooks in the congregation. "Annie," he said, inclining his head. "How you doin' today?"

"Just fine. And you?"

"Good as gold. Mr. Corbin said you'd be comin' by and to tell you to come through the glass door at the front."

"Thanks, Early. See you in church tomorrow?"

"Sure will. Don't miss one. Can't afford to." He smiled and directed her through the gate.

Annie's stomach had been in knots since she'd gotten out of bed this morning. In the wake of everything else that had happened last night, she hadn't given a lot of analysis to the reason Jack had wanted to see her. But while she straightened the house and greeted each of the boys' mothers when they came to pick them up, curiosity had her willing the clock forward.

She followed the road to the front of the factory where Early had indicated she should park, punching off the classical music station she'd turned on in an effort to soothe her anxiety.

She got out of the Tahoe, a breeze catching the hem of her lightweight coat and blowing it out behind her. The air had a nip to it this morning, a precursor to

the cold front predicted to move in by evening, low-
ering temperatures into the fifties by dawn.

Annie climbed the steps to the glass door now,
wondering if she should knock or just go in. But the
door opened, and Jack stood in front of her, looking
like the unsmiling twin brother of the man who'd
been giving pony rides to the group of boys at her
house last night.

"Morning," he said.

"Hi," she said, his seriousness giving her opti-
mism good cause for concern.

"Come on in, Annie," he said, and stepped aside
to let her enter. He indicated the way with one hand,
letting her lead with the good manners that so far
were consistent with him. J.D. had been the kind of
guy who pulled a chair out for a woman if someone
else was looking.

"Take a right down the next hallway," Jack said.

From the corner of her eye, Annie thought she saw
his gaze drop over her. Had he just checked her out?
Her face grew warm, and she did an instant checklist
of all the things he could have been noticing: Cyrus's
ever-shedding hair on her pants, a spot the dry cleaner
had missed.

Or maybe he was just checking her out.

That's what it had felt like.

Wrong, Annie.

Men like Jack didn't lust after women like her.
She'd never really thought of herself as the kind of

woman to inspire lust, period. But definitely not in a man like this one.

The hallway dead-ended.

"This is my father's old office," Jack said.

Annie nodded, her voice having decided not to make an appearance yet. It was a handsome room, a lot of big furniture, cherry wood, but most noticeable were the dozens of family pictures adorning the walls and desktop. A lot of them were of Jack, as a boy, as a teenager. Those early versions had hinted well at the man to come.

"Sit down," he said, going around to the other end of the desk on which stacks of folders were piled up like snowdrifts. "I actually came back here after I left your house last night."

"You've been here since then?"

"I went home this morning to shower and inject a few cups of coffee."

Annie nodded, noticing that he'd called Glenn Hall home. Was he beginning to think of it that way again? "So what is all this?"

"That's what I'm trying to figure out. I'm still not sure."

The assertion stood for a few moments until Annie finally said, "And what is it I can help you with?"

He got up and closed the door. Back at the desk, he said, "I was hoping you could answer a few things for me, Annie. I didn't want to ask any of the employees and get everyone stirred up when there very well may be no reason for it."

"I'll do my best," she said, crossing her legs and sitting straighter in her chair. Uneasiness thumped its presence against the wall of her chest. Her palms began to sweat.

"I've been looking at the financial statements for the past six years. Starting after my father died," he said.

Jack sat down in the leather chair behind the desk. "What can you tell me about Hugh Kroner?"

"He's your controller, right?"

"Yes."

Annie drew in a deep breath. "Let's see. He and his family go to my church. I think he has three girls in college. His wife does a lot of volunteer work in the county. I don't know either of them very well, but they seem like good people."

Jack nodded. And then threw out several other names, three of whom she knew well enough to comment on, two she did not.

While she talked, he made some notes on the yellow legal pad in front of him.

He touched a hand to some papers on his desk. "The thing that keeps jumping out at me is the size of the inventory adjustment made each month."

She waved a hand in the air. "Non-business person aboard."

"Each month the company conducts a physical inventory count and compares that to the computer's numbers. It's normal for a slight adjustment to be made when the numbers don't match. But the differences here are unusually high. And it looks as if over the last year or so, they've gotten even higher."

"So does that mean someone's stealing inventory?"

"Possibly."

"Is there a way to dig deeper?"

"Yes. By looking at the inventory counts and adjustments in detail. For example, the physical inventory might say we had ninety-five dining room tables and the computer says we had one hundred."

"That means five are missing," she said.

"Right."

"How many months have you looked at?"

"I've just pulled out several at random from the past few years."

"Could we take a look at each month? I'd love to help."

"I'm talking about hours and hours of work, Annie. I couldn't ask—"

"I want to," she said, standing, imploring him to see she meant it. She'd do a twenty-four hour shift if it meant giving this company a chance to survive. "Can we start now?"

"You must have other things to do."

"Nothing that can't wait. And Mrs. Parker, my regular sitter, is at the house with Tommy. So really, I'm at your disposal."

Jack studied her for several moments that felt like minutes. Her cheeks grew warm under the perusal. She was vividly aware of the minimal makeup she'd put on that morning. When was the last time she'd plucked her eyebrows? Was the lighting that good in here? Why hadn't she straightened her hair with the blow-dryer instead of letting it go its own maddening way?

"If you're sure, Annie—"

"I'm sure."

BY TWO O'CLOCK that afternoon, they were up to their elbows in files and computer printouts. Annie's lower back had begun to ache from sitting in one spot for so long. A wonder the company hadn't sunk long ago from the sheer weight of the paperwork involved to keep it running.

It didn't take long to figure out that he had a mind like a computer program. A single glance at a column of figures usually told him what he needed to know, and they were on to the next printout.

Annie worked at the keyboard, bringing up the next month's inventory count when he asked for it, waiting while he made notes on his legal pad and asked for certain ones to be printed out.

"Is this the kind of thing you do in your work?" Annie asked while they were waiting for one of the longer files to print.

"Sometimes. It kind of varies depending on the situation," he said. "It's a little bit like detective work. You have to go in and figure out what's causing the problems. Sometimes it's pretty evident to someone from the outside with no bias. And sometimes it's not.''

"Do you have a main office?"

"In D.C. I started a consulting business with one of my buddies from graduate school. We rack up a lot of frequent flyer miles. The companies we work for are all over the place.''

"You don't mind all that traveling?"

"Not too much. Doesn't make for real stable housekeeping.''

"Footloose and—"

"—fancy free," he finished for her.

Annie smiled, even as an inexplicable pang of disappointment hit her. Sometimes it was no fun being right.

"It's good work," he said. "I change projects often enough to not get bored. We just got a long-term project in London, actually. I'm scheduled to head there after I'm done here.''

"Oh. Wow. But how can you—" She waved a hand at the stacks of paper surrounding them, not sure how to finish her question.

"I don't know, Annie. Right now, I'm just following my curiosity. It may not take us anywhere but right back to my decision that closing the company is for the best.''

At three o'clock, they took a break. Jack went in search of a drink machine, and Annie called Mrs. Parker to see if she could stay on for a while longer.

"Of course. Take your time, Annie," the other

woman said. "I don't have anywhere else to be, and Tommy is perfectly happy playing with all his birthday presents."

Annie hung up the phone and said a silent prayer of thanks for Mrs. Parker.

"This okay?" Jack was back, a bottle of water in each hand.

"Perfect," she said. "Thank you."

They got right back to work, their efforts peppered with very little personal conversation. To Annie, it felt as if Jack was trying to keep the afternoon on a purely business footing. Not that she'd expected anything different, but the change from last night was noticeable. Feeling the shift, Annie kept her own comments on target with the task at hand, corraling back into the chute any thoughts that might attempt to stray toward the fact that he had the kind of strong hands she'd always liked on a man, or that she found the subtle lemony scent of his aftershave appealing.

They didn't stop again until almost seven o'clock. By then, they had covered most of a tabletop with printouts Jack wanted to take a closer look at.

"That'll take days to go through, won't it?"

"I can get through it pretty quickly," he said.

"You and what army?"

He smiled. "I'm used to running solo."

Double entendre there, or was she just looking for it? Annie sat back in her chair and ran a hand through what she knew was seriously deflated hair. She felt faded, wilted, wrinkled and about as attractive as a woman who'd been standing out in the rain waiting for a bus. Good thing she wasn't interested in him. Even so, vanity pleaded with her to do a powder-room check. Okay, so she did have her pride.

She stood, held up a finger. "Ladies' room."

He nodded and said, "I think this is plenty for tonight, anyway."

The damage, when she got in front of the mirror to assess it, was worse than she'd feared. Good heavens, how was it possible to go downhill so fast? Her hair had, indeed, deflated, and she could have lit Bowers' Stadium with the shine on her nose.

What difference does it make, Annie? In a few short days, you'll likely never see this man again. The argument, valid as it was, did not prevent her from pulling out a brush and compact to repair the damage. When she'd finished, the mirror reflected back a more acceptable version of herself. At least she could go back out and say goodbye without ducking her head.

Jack was waiting for her at the door to the office, flipping off the light inside and saying, "Dinner. My treat. I insist."

"You don't have to do that. Really. I was glad to help out. I just hope you learn something that might make a difference."

"I'm starving. You have to be hungry, too," he said, avoiding her statement like a professional skater zipping around a chink in the ice.

"I'm fine, actually," she began just as her stomach

sounded out a noisy rumble, making an instant liar of her.

Jack smiled. "See."

"Okay, let me just make sure Mrs. Parker can stay."

SO HE SHOULD HAVE SAID, "Thanks for the help, Annie," and let her be on her way.

That would have been the reasonable thing to do. Logical, anyway. No point in edging into something that had no chance of ever developing into more.

That said, what harm could there be in two adults having a quick dinner after spending most of a day working together?

A quick discussion in the C.M. parking lot had led them to agree on a place just outside of town called Lugar's. It was new to the area, Annie had said, but they served a little bit of everything, and the food was good. Standing beside her at the entrance to the restaurant, Jack wondered if one of its merits had also been location and that they were less likely to see anyone she knew out here. Had it been true, he wouldn't have really blamed her. He was the town's current black sheep and didn't plan on hanging around long enough to be bothered by whether anyone liked him or not, but the same was not true for Annie.

If people saw them together, there would be talk.

Regardless of Annie's reasons for picking it, the place seemed like a good choice. From the front door, the smells were paralyzingly good, the lighting low enough to be appealing, a glass window at the back of the restaurant showing off a stainless steel kitchen and two cooks in tall white hats.

"Fancy," Jack said when the waitress had left them at their table near the center of the room.

"The food really is wonderful. Clarice did a story on them when they first opened here. The owners moved down from New York. They had a successful restaurant somewhere up there. They were robbed one night after closing, their son shot and nearly killed. They didn't want to live like that anymore and started looking for a smaller place where things like that didn't happen so often."

And Macon's Point was that kind of place. Over the years, Jack had let himself forget its appeal, living for the most part in big cities, places where the newspapers were filled with stories like those Annie had just described. He appreciated for the first time since he'd left this town the fact that the *County Times* was more likely to feature a local farmer's cows getting out than the daily laundry list of murder and mayhem he had grown so used to seeing that he no longer really saw it anymore.

Wasn't there something wrong with a life where that kind of thing no longer shocked?

The waitress came back with their menus, and they spent a couple of minutes in silent perusal, the question still tugging at Jack. When she returned to see if they were ready, Annie ordered a salad and the roasted chicken, the house specialty. Jack opted for the same and pointed out a bottle of white wine to go with it.

Once the waitress headed toward the kitchen with their orders, he leaned back in his chair and folded his arms across his chest. "What made you want to be mayor, Annie?"

She considered the question. "In all honesty, maybe at first a need to do a better job than J.D. had. But at some point, it became about wanting to do good things for this town. I'm not naive. I know a lot of people think I'm kind of a joke."

Jack thought about the two men he'd overheard at the picnic and resented their unfairness. "From everything I've seen, you take what you do seriously."

"I guess people make their own interpretations of a situation sometimes. You just have to hope that eventually your intentions show through and people are willing to recognize them."

"So what else made you stay here, Annie?"

She fiddled with the stem on her water glass. "The sense of community, I think," she said. "I've never felt a part of a place the way I do now. As if I'm not just another cog in the wheel. For the most part, people here care about each other. There's just this feeling of welcome I've never known anywhere else. That's why Clarice ended up staying. That and the fact that she's crazy about Tommy."

That was the second time she'd mentioned Clarice since they'd sat down. Jack had a feeling Annie was making a deliberate effort to keep her sister's name between them. "You two are close, aren't you?"

"Best friends. Our parents were killed in a car wreck a few years ago. We're kind of all the other one has."

Surprise left him without words. "I'm sorry, Annie," he said, hearing the flimsiness of his response and yet unable to think of anything else to say.

"Thank you. It's one of those things you never expect to hear."

"And certainly not to lose them both at once."

"No. It puts things into perspective pretty quickly. I learned the hard way that you should never let things go unsaid, unfinished. There may not be another opportunity other than the here and now."

Jack thought of his own father, of how he'd never forgiven him, never patched things up. Something that felt like regret hit him low in the gut, its edge painful. For so many years, his feelings about his father had been set in concrete, completely unyielding. And with his return to the place where he'd grown up, it was as if a crack had appeared, letting in the slightest sliver of light, making him question his choices.

He put his focus back on the woman sitting across from him. "Mind if I ask how you got to Macon's Point?"

Annie shook her head. "After J.D. could no longer play ball, he was kind of at loose ends. One of the town council members called and asked him to consider the position. I think he looked at it as kind of a lark. Something to take on while he waited for his shoulder to heal.''

''Except it didn't.''

''No.''

''What caused the injury?''

''It was actually an old water-skiing injury. Arthritis set up in the joint, and surgery didn't help.''

''A shame. He was a good ballplayer.''

''He lived for it.''

Something in her voice told him that was all J.D. lived for.

''Did you two know each other?'' she asked.

''By sight. We went to different schools, and he was a few years older.''

''Oh.''

''So Clarice moved here after you did?''

Annie nodded. ''We both always loved small towns. She came to visit one weekend after J.D. and I moved here and fell in love with it. So when he left, she decided to fill the vacancy.''

''What about J.D.'s parents?''

''They moved to Arizona not long after we moved here. The winters had gotten too long for them. We usually see them once a year or so when they come through on a R. V. trip.'' She shrugged. ''I guess it's kind of odd that I ended up staying when it was J.D.'s hometown to begin with, but—''

''Sounds like Langor County won out on that one.''

Annie smiled and looked pleased by the compliment. Which technically, it was. But fact, too, he had a feeling.

"I'm not sure it was the best thing for Clarice's social life. She spends far too much time with Tommy for a woman attempting the dating scene. But he adores her, and it's hard for me to push her out the front door when she shows up with pizza on a Friday night."

Jack smiled. Okay, so she was pitching her sister to him and he wasn't sure how he felt about that. Clarice was a very attractive woman, and from surface appearances, she was the type he normally would have asked out. So why was he sitting here at this table across from her sister who, from everything he'd seen so far, was definitely not his type? And how did he explain the pull he felt toward her?

The waitress came back then with two glasses and the bottle of wine. She uncorked it with admirable ease, asked if they were both having some, and at their dual nods, poured for each of them.

Annie took a sip. "Mmm, that's good. Crisp."

"Good vineyard. I actually did some work for them out in the Napa Valley. Fairly small family business. Dedicated to making quality wine that regular people can afford."

"You've really been all over the place, haven't you?"

"Here and there. It was one of the things I found appealing about the kind of work I do. Seeing the world. I mean find appealing," he corrected himself, wondering at his own slip.

Annie nodded as if she understood, when her expression clearly said the opposite. "We traveled a lot when J.D. was playing ball."

"You miss that?"

"No," she said, so quickly that there was no missing the truth behind the statement. "I felt like I was always waiting for life to begin, that the next town would be the one where we really put down roots. Not that I'm complaining," she added quickly. "I know a lot of people would find that kind of life exciting."

"You just didn't."

She shook her head. "This is plenty of excitement for me."

He nodded understanding. The truth was just a few days ago he didn't think he would have understood. Maybe he hadn't allowed himself to remember the good stuff about Macon's Point because he'd known he was never going to live here again. But he did remember a lot of it now, was seeing it for himself, and he couldn't deny its appeal. He knew as surely as he was sitting here that Annie was right about the fact that closing C.M. would change the quality of life in Langor County. A sudden urge to keep that from happening hit him dead center.

"Tell me what it was like growing up here," Annie said, her wineglass cupped between both hands, a look of sincere interest on her face.

"We spent a lot of time outdoors. My dad and I. He used to take me hiking up on Carver's Knob. You could see just about the whole county from up there."

"Really?" Annie's eyes lit with interest. "I've never been there."

"The views are incredible."

"You were close to your father," she said.

"At one time."

"What happened?" she asked, her voice soft, threaded with concern.

Jack shrugged his best I-don't-know-it-doesn't-really-matter-anyway shrug and said, "He changed after Mom died."

"How so?"

"He married his secretary three months after the funeral."

Sympathy flitted across Annie's face, for him or the situation, he wasn't sure. But it made him want to change the direction of the conversation, fast. "That's all water under the bridge."

"Still hurts, though."

He looked up, caught the caring look in her eyes. Something inside him flipped over, like a door opening that was never going to close the same way again.

"Yeah, pretty much puts to rest any such notions as love lasting forever," he said, going for flip and coming off way closer to sincere.

"Do you doubt that he loved your mother?"

Jack shook his head. "No. But it must not have been in the way I always believed it to be."

"How was that?"

"Maybe all children think this of their parents, but I guess I just thought what they had was special. Different from the way a lot of my friends' parents loved each other. My dad got this look in his eyes whenever Mom walked in a room. It was," he hesitated, searching for the right word, "like relief that she'd come back. Like what they had was so good that it couldn't last forever. Turns out it didn't."

"What happened to your mother?" The question was little more than a whisper.

Jack looked up, met Annie's gaze, the compassion there tightening the clamp on his own heart. "She used to do volunteer work at a nursing home on Tuesday afternoons. Visiting with the patients who didn't have anyone else to come see them. She had this Great Dane, Maude, she always took with her." He looked away from Annie's intense gaze, feeling for a moment as if she could see inside him. "It started sleeting on her way home one afternoon. She slid off a curve and hit a tree just a mile from our house. My dad had gotten worried about her and left work to come home. He found them—"

Jack stopped there, the rest of the sentence stuck in his throat. To that point, the words had come out neutral, as if he were some impartial bystander telling the story. But he felt the layers of his own self-protection begin to slip away, and he could not say any more.

Annie reached across the table, took his hand and

held it between the two of hers. Her cheeks were wet with tears. "I'm sorry, Jack. She sounds like a lovely woman."

He swallowed, nodding. Tried to respond and couldn't. It had been so long since he'd talked about his mother. He never did. Never. It was just easier not to because even after all these years, both the pain of losing her and the changes that loss had brought to his life were still right there on the surface. So why was he sitting here with Annie telling her things he'd never told anyone else? What was it about her that made him feel it was safe to do so?

"I didn't mean to get into all that," he said, finally recovering his voice.

"Your mother was lucky to have a son who still misses her. That says something about the kind of person she was."

"She was a good woman."

Annie looked at him for a long moment. "Why did you never come back to Macon's Point?"

"My dad started a new life after Mom died. We never really saw eye to eye on that." He looked down, moved his silverware around. "Maybe I expected too much. My parents' marriage made me think that sometimes people were just made for each other. That maybe they were born on certain paths that were meant to cross at some point. And that once they found one another there would never be anyone else."

"And you don't believe that anymore?"

"No, I don't," he said, looking up to meet the disappointment in her eyes.

"Is that why you've never married?"

The directness of the question knocked him off balance for a moment. "Got as close as almost. And I ended up hurting a very nice woman who did not deserve to be hurt."

She considered that for a moment. "I'm sorry to hear that. But I guess I do believe certain people are meant to meet. That it's not all just random."

And sitting there across from a woman for whom such a thing ought to be true, Jack wished like hell he could tell her he was wrong.

CHAPTER EIGHT

HE HAD INSISTED on following her home.

Annie had told him she would be fine, really. But he wouldn't hear of anything other than making sure she got there safely. And, well, she couldn't deny she was a sucker for chivalry. Since it rarely ever came along in her everyday life, its appearance was hard to resist.

All the way home, Annie thought about Jack's jaded views on lasting love. So maybe that explained his less-than-sterling reputation for packing up camp at the first sight of anything remotely close to serious.

In the back of her mind, warnings were going up like emergency flares. He had just told her he didn't believe in any of the things that she refused to discard as so much romantic notion. And his conviction ran deep enough to be of the permanent variety.

Still, she pulled into the circular driveway with his headlights reflecting in her rearview mirror, more than a little thrilled by his gallantry.

Stop, Annie. She put the Tahoe in park, turned off the engine and removed the keys with a hand that wasn't quite steady. Not the wine, either. She'd only had one glass. No, this was intoxication of another

sort altogether. And without doubt, far more dangerous to the strands of independence that held together
her very ordinary life. It was just that she wasn't used
to such treatment.

She got out of her own car just as Jack pulled in
behind her and cut his headlights.

"I noticed there wasn't another car here. Does your
sitter need a ride home?"

"Her car was in the shop so I picked her up this
morning," Annie said. "I'll take her home. It's just
a couple miles."

"Well, I'm headed back, anyway," he said. "Be
glad to do it."

"Are you sure?"

"Absolutely."

"Come on in, then," she said, tipping her head
toward the house.

He got out and followed her to the door. The front
porch light was on, and she sent a quick glance at
him while she fished through her purse for her house
keys which somehow always made their way to the
bottom like rocks in a pond.

"Thank you," she said. "I'm sure Tommy is already asleep, so I'd have to wake him up to take Mrs.
Parker."

"Glad to do it."

Standing there under the light on her porch, Annie
felt his gaze on her. She looked up with the strangest
sense of inevitability, as if this were a moment she'd
been waiting for. Awareness snapped between them.

Sharp and undeniable. Purely physical. Annie felt it zing through her like an arrow aimed directly at her heart, the place where all feeling began. From there, it began a slow seep outward, tingling its way up through her chest, down her spine and then a quick, heady rush through arms and legs. And it was one of those moments when a woman knows, just knows somehow, that a man wants to kiss her as much as she wants him to do it.

The front door opened. The moment shattered like glass on granite.

"I thought I heard you pull in." Mrs. Parker stood just inside the foyer, her oval-rimmed glasses half-askew as if she'd just shoved them on. "I must have dozed off on the couch."

"I'm sorry it's so late," Annie said. "We stopped for a quick dinner. Mrs. Parker, this is Jack Corbin. Jack, Lydia Parker."

"Nice to meet you, Mr. Corbin."

"Jack, please. And it's nice to meet you. Thought I'd offer you a ride home if you'd like."

Mrs. Parker raised an eyebrow at Annie. "Well, now, I sure didn't expect to end my day riding home with a handsome stranger."

Annie smiled and knew just how the older woman felt. "Some days end with nice surprises, don't they?"

"Some days do," Mrs. Parker said.

THEY HADN'T GOTTEN a quarter mile down the road when the older woman said, "So you're the young man Annie's trying to convince not to close down Corbin Manufacturing.''

"Yes, ma'am,'' Jack said, wishing he could have hung another identity on himself.

"Is she?''

Jack threw her a glance. "What's that?''

"Convincing you?''

Nothing like directness to put a hitch in a man's step. From all appearances, Lydia Parker was a sweet, gray-haired grandmotherly type. It looked as though he was going to get a quick tutorial that when it came to Annie, her protective feathers could get ruffled pretty easily.

And he liked her for it. Wasn't too sure he appreciated her opening that front door at the precise moment she had, but maybe that had turned out to be a good thing. Because if she hadn't, he'd still be back there on that porch kissing Annie. There was just no denying that fact.

"I'm not too sure how things are going to turn out with the factory, Mrs. Parker. We'll just have to wait and see. But yes, Annie's had some very convincing arguments for trying to revive it.''

"You know there aren't a lot of women around like that one these days.''

"She takes her job seriously,'' he agreed, not sure where he was supposed to go with this.

"Yes, she does. Unlike that skunk of a husband she had.''

On this, Jack hoped she would elaborate.

"Any man that would run off and leave a woman and child like those two—" She broke off there, shaking her head, her opinion as clearly expressed as if she'd gone on for another hour reciting all the bad things that should happen to J. D. McCabe.

"Maybe he didn't realize what he had."

"No doubt about that," she said with a nod.

"She'd be just fine if she raised that boy on her own. But she deserves a good man in her life. It's my hope she'll find one. Or he'll find her."

Had Mrs. Parker been looking out the window before she'd opened that door a few minutes ago? Jack's guess was yes.

"I sure would hate, though, to see her get her hopes up for something that didn't have a chance. It's taken a long time for her to get over the batch of hurt that J.D. left her with. She's not one to let on to many people, but I saw it with my own eyes."

"Annie's lucky to have someone who cares about her the way you do," Jack said, wondering if he should be offended that he was being alluded to in the same breath that Annie's ex-husband was being taken down with.

"Not a lot of work to it," Mrs. Parker said. "Turn right just past that barn. That's my driveway."

Jack slowed, flipped on his signal light and made the turn onto the gravel road. They drove another half mile or so before coming to a two-story brick house with twin pecan trees in the front yard.

"Thank you," she said. "I appreciate the ride. I hope Annie's efforts pay off."

"Good night, Mrs. Parker," he said, not sure what else to say. He waited while she unlocked her front door and let herself in with a wave.

Driving home a few minutes later, Jack thought about what the older woman had said. Not a lot of work to it. And he had to admit that she was right. If a man believed in such notions as love and commitment, it would be hard not to fall for a woman like Annie.

If a man believed in that sort of thing.

THE PHONE WAS RINGING when Jack walked into the kitchen at Glenn Hall a few minutes later. A renegade hope that it might be Annie was his only explanation for the speed with which he snapped up the cordless phone.

"Jack? It's Clarice. I hope I'm not calling too late."

"No," he said, surprised.

"I was wondering if you'd like to come over for dinner tomorrow night."

"Dinner," he said, stalling and not at all sure where to go with this.

"I promise it'll be good. Annie said she'll supervise. She's the cook in the family. I defer all judgment to her."

Annie's sister had just asked him out. So Annie

had known she was going to? That explained, then, the frequent insertion of Clarice's name at dinner.

It did not explain the fact that he'd almost kissed Annie less than an hour ago, and unless his intuition on such things had gone haywire, she'd wanted him to do so.

Apparently, his intuition had gone haywire.

Disappointment fell over him like thunderheads. Okay, so wrong read on that. Maybe his antennae were a little off, and what he'd imagined back there on Annie's porch had been one-sided altogether. That acknowledged, maybe having dinner with Clarice would be the exact thing to derail his growing attraction to her sister. "What time should I be there, Clarice?"

SUNDAY DAWNED crisp and clear, a beautiful early fall day. Annie swung out of bed, something inside her feeling equally renewed.

Jack had nearly kissed her.

Or at least she'd thought he was going to.

He'd wanted to, hadn't he?

For the duration of her shower, Annie told herself not to be foolish. *Feet on the ground, Annie McCabe.*

She got out, anchored a towel around herself and rubbed steam from the vanity mirror. There was something that looked way too much like infatuation in her eyes.

The recognition brought with it a list of reasons for a reality check.

She took the list with her downstairs to the kitchen where she pulled coffee beans from the freezer. The phone rang. She picked it up and tucked it under her chin, pouring beans into the grinder. "Hello."

"Iaskedhimovertodinnerhesaidyescanyouhelpmefix-somethinggreat?"

"Clarice?"

"I'm desperate! I need your help."

"You asked—"

"Jack."

"Jack."

"I kind of fudged and told him you said you'd help. I'll owe you big."

Annie dropped her head back and stared at the ceiling for a moment with lips pressed together. Told herself she was an idiot. "You won't owe me, Clarice," she said, her voice even, despite what felt like a very large lump in her throat. "I'll be glad to help."

"And you don't mind? That I asked him, I mean?"

"Of course not. Why would I mind?"

"Annie, you're the best. Okay, I've got to run by the office before church. I'll see you there. Maybe we can go to the grocery store afterward?"

"Sure, Clarice." Annie hung up the phone and put away the coffee beans, a few pins of sibling rivalry pricking at her skin. What was she supposed to say, though? *No, Clarice. You can't have him over for dinner because I thought he might kiss me last night, and I really wanted him to.*

Clarice's call should not have come as a surprise,

but it left Annie feeling as though someone had knocked the wind from her sails. Because there was no denying that she'd gone to bed last night walking just a couple inches off the ground, ridiculously buoyed by what she now saw as no more than a moment of awareness between her and a man with whom she'd spent a very pleasant evening. A moment where she'd been sure he was going to kiss her, and she had wanted him to.

A memory echoed through her, one she'd thought long ago tucked away. The only major disagreement she ever remembered Clarice and her having. Over a boy, at that. Clarice had been in the tenth grade, Annie in the ninth. They'd been at a new school again that year. On the very first day, Annie had fallen stone dead in love with Craig Overby. Her locker was right next to his, and he'd struck up a conversation with her when he'd caught her staring at him, as discreetly as a ninth-grader could stare at a star football player with a face that drew girls like a magnet did steel.

For two days, Annie had lived for visits to her locker. Each time she saw him they talked a little longer, and Annie had the kind of crush on him that makes it impossible to eat, sleep or think.

And then on the third day, Clarice came by to see Annie between classes. Annie just happened to be looking when Craig spotted her sister. His eyeballs all but fell out of his head. And that was pretty much that. Clarice's reaction to him had been the same as Annie's, the only difference being that within three days, they were holding hands and kissing beside Annie's locker.

Annie had never been angry with her sister before. But fury boiled inside her, until one night after supper, her father noticed that the two girls weren't talking and confronted them.

"All right, you two, what seems to be the problem?"

"Annie's mad at me because she thinks I stole her boyfriend," Clarice had explained as if she were telling him Annie thought she'd taken the grapes out of her lunchbox.

"Did you?"

"She might have thought he was her boyfriend! But Craig said he felt sorry for her because she was new and he was just being friendly!"

Something inside Annie had collapsed with the words. Humiliation coursed through her, hot, scalding. "Craig Overby is a jerk, and you're welcome to him!" she'd said with less-than-believable vehemence.

"He is not a jerk! You're just jealous!" Clarice had cried.

"Go to your room, Clarice," their father had ordered.

"But Daddy—"

"Now."

Clarice's exit had left Annie alone to face her father's disappointed head-shaking. "Annie, I don't like seeing you girls fight over a boy. You're awfully young for that.''

"He was my friend, Daddy, until Clarice came along.''

Her father sighed and sat down on the couch beside her, putting his arm around her shoulders. "You'll probably find this hard to believe now, honey, but my brother Ed was always the looker in the family. From the time he was in nursery school, girls flocked after him like he was the Pied Piper. Anytime Ed was around, I felt like a shadow, just kind of in the background. And of course one year when we were in high school, I developed a crush on this girl I actually thought I had a chance with. Until she saw Ed.''

He tilted his head at her, the meaning behind the words clear. "I was so mad at my brother I could hardly see straight for days. But then I finally realized it wasn't Ed's fault. He didn't try to take her away from me. She just preferred him, and there was nothing I could do about that. I decided then and there, though, I was never going to compete with my brother over a girl. No girl was worth the two of us fighting over. Luckily, your mother thought I was the better pick of the litter, and Ed never had a chance with her.''

A wink accompanied this, and Annie tried to smile.

"You're a special girl, honey. Selfless and loyal. And one day a man is going to come along who appreciates those qualities.''

At fourteen, Annie had understood what her father

was trying to say as painlessly as he could. There were some things in life a person just had to accept. The fact that Clarice had been born movie-star beautiful was one of them. The fact that Annie had not, another.

For Annie, like her father, the lesson that day had been never to compete with her sister again. It just wasn't all that smart to start battles you had no chance of winning.

Besides, she told herself, shaking off the past, Clarice was the one who really wanted a man in her life now. Who'd been waiting for the right one to come along. Macon's Point wasn't exactly overflowing with eligible men. Clarice spent so much of her free time with Annie and Tommy, anyway. Far too much for a single woman looking to get married.

So what if she'd wanted to be kissed last night? Nothing abnormal about that. Just her heart's way of telling her maybe it was time to start going out again. She was a young, healthy woman with normal wants and desires who just happened to have had them flattened by her ex-husband's cheating. At least she knew they still existed.

She could thank Jack for proving that much, anyway.

And if Clarice wanted him, then Annie would be her biggest champion for the cause. She pulled her favorite cookbook from the shelf on the kitchen island and began looking for something he might like.

CHAPTER NINE

SUNDAY MORNING SERVICE at Macon's Point First Baptist began at eleven. It was the only church Annie had ever been to where there was actually standing room only at quarter till. The church, with its wonderful old stained-glass windows, was some hundred and fifty years old and sat smack in the center of town. It had been one of the first buildings erected by the area's early citizens, and the town, as it was to become, grew outward from here. When she'd first learned its history, Annie had appreciated the symbolism. Because from the beginning, she had felt the deep roots of faith in this community, proof of its existence plain to see in the pews filled shoulder to shoulder. It was the kind of church Annie had always wanted to be a part of, with its strong sense of community and goodwill.

"Mama, where's Aunt Clarice?" Tommy looked up from the bulletin he'd been folding into a fan.

"She must be running a little late this morning."

No sooner had Annie said the words than Clarice appeared beside them, breathless but smiling. "Hey," she said, voice lowered. "Can I climb over?"

"Sure," Annie said, letting her sister squeeze by to sit on the other side of Tommy.

Clarice gave him a smooch on the forehead. "What's up, scooter?"

Tommy smiled and said, "Nothing, Aunt Clarice."

"Nothing? Goodness, that's boring."

Annie smiled at their teasing.

Clarice's eyes suddenly went wide.

"What?" Annie said.

"He's here!"

Annie turned to follow her sister's surprised gaze. On the other side of the aisle was Jack Corbin sitting next to Essie Poindexter. No sooner had Annie spotted him than he looked up, catching the two of them staring. Heat torched Annie's face, why she wasn't sure. Embarrassment for having been caught staring or her own awareness of attraction and her very real hope that it did not show on her face? Either way, she gave a quick wave and as impersonal a smile as she could muster.

"Oh, my heart, Annie," Clarice stage-whispered. "He's wearing a suit! Does he look good in that or what?"

"I'm wearing a suit, Aunt Clarice," Tommy chimed in.

"You certainly are, handsome devil," she said.

Tommy grinned, old enough to appreciate his aunt's adoration.

Annie reached for a hymnal and turned to the first song listed on the board to the right of the pulpit, trying not to look as flustered as she felt. She had not expected to see Jack here this morning. Her insides felt as if they'd suffered a small earthquake, and her hands shook a little where they gripped the songbook.

Annie…

The self-chiding might be deserved, but the truth was her reaction to Jack Corbin was not something she had any control over. She couldn't obliterate its existence altogether, but she could ignore it. Which she pointedly set out to do.

The choir director stepped up to the podium and raised a hand for everyone to stand. The piano and organ struck up with one of Annie's favorites, "Just As I Am," and she turned her focus to the song's poignant strains.

Was it her imagination, or did she feel Jack's gaze from across the aisle? And why was it that among all the others in the congregation, she singled out his voice following the music, rich and deep?

ANNIE AND TOMMY pulled into the parking lot of Kinley's Grocery just before one that afternoon. After the service, Clarice had hung back to say hello to Jack and tell him she was looking forward to tonight. Annie had said she and Tommy were going on so they could make a quick stop at the Dairy Queen to get some lunch.

"Why are we helping Aunt Clarice grocery shop?" Tommy asked when they were headed toward Kinley's.

"She's cooking a special dinner tonight and wants some advice on what to fix."

"Doesn't she know how to cook, Mama?"

"Some things," Annie said. "She's just never taken a lot of interest in it."

"Is that why the cake she made me that time wasn't very tall?"

"I think she forgot to put the baking soda in it."

"Oh. I like them better with baking soda."

"Don't tell Aunt Clarice that."

"I won't. It'd hurt her feelings."

Kinley's was the kind of old-fashioned grocery store disappearing from small towns like minnows being swallowed up by much bigger fish. It had its own bakery, the smells greeting customers at the front door, no sales pitch needed. Their meat department was so top-notch that people came weekly from two counties away just to buy their first-quality steaks and the fresh trout raised on a farm in Langor County.

Clarice was standing in the produce department looking like someone who'd jumped in a swimming pool only to realize she couldn't swim. She looked up, spotted them, waved. "Help!"

"You haven't even gotten out of fruits and vegetables yet," Annie said, smiling.

"There are four hundred kinds of lettuce in here." She gave Tommy a hug and said, "Forgot to pay you for cleaning out my car the other day."

Tommy gave her an I-didn't-forget-about-it nod.

"He's way too shrewd for a seven-year-old," Clarice said to Annie.

"I know."

Clarice reached in her purse, pulled out the five dollars they'd agreed on. "I'm surprised you didn't tack on interest for late payment."

His smile said he'd thought about it.

"Way too shrewd," Clarice said again, shaking her head.

"Thanks, Aunt Clarice," Tommy said. "Mama, can I go look at the comic books?"

"Sure, doodles, but remember—"

"Half in my piggy bank, I know," he said.

"Didn't think he'd forget that rule, did you, Annie? He'll be starting his own mutual fund by the time he's ten."

Annie laughed, watching Tommy trot down the produce aisle to the other end of the store where the comic books were displayed. She was proud of how responsible Tommy already was. The effort had been deliberate on her part. She'd wanted to teach him the value of saving. It wasn't something J.D. had ever believed in, and he'd somehow managed to go through most of the money he'd earned playing ball (she still wondered where it could have all gone) so that now he'd been reduced to spokeperson ads for fast food fried chicken.

"Thank you for coming," Clarice said, giving Annie a hug. "I know I'm ridiculous."

"It's not ridiculous," Annie said.

"Hey, I'm the one who called the Butterball hotline last Thanksgiving, remember?"

"Three times," Annie said, the memory making her laugh until she felt weak.

"You snorted!" Clarice accused.

"Did not."

"Did, too!"

"Come on, Julia, why don't we start with the lettuce?"

"Annie, you're a lifesaver."

LIFESAVER ANNIE DROVE home late that afternoon feeling like the world's biggest hypocrite. She'd put a good face on helping Clarice with her dinner, but deep down, something that could only be identified as jealousy simmered like a bitter brew. She'd helped out with the meal Clarice had planned like Santa's best elf packing up all the toys, which made her envy all the uglier.

And she disliked herself intensely for it.

Clarice had a date with Jack tonight. That was that. And in all likelihood, he'd walk away as smitten as every other man who ever came under Clarice's spell. She was going at it full throttle. He didn't have a chance.

So get over it, Annie.

She looked at Tommy who was deep into one of the comic books he'd bought at Kinley's. "What do you think about going to a movie tonight?"

Tommy shot a fist in the air. "All right! Can we get popcorn?"

"The largest bucket they have," Annie said.

"What are we gonna see?"

"Whatever you want."

The pleased smile on her son's face filled her with gratitude. She was so lucky to have him. Lucky to be living in a place she thought her son would one day be proud to call his hometown. So she might yen for companionship now and then. For all the negatives of her marriage to J.D., Tommy made the enduring of every one of them worthwhile.

She didn't need a crystal ball to tell her the unwiseness of dwelling on her attraction to Jack. So the very sight of him ignited a physical reaction inside her she'd never felt before. So she'd thought for sure he was going to kiss her last night. So he made Tommy laugh the kind of belly laugh little boys have a right to.

So…he had a date with her sister tonight. And that made all the rest null and void.

CLARICE HADN'T BEEN this nervous since her first prom in high school. She glanced at the clock beside the fireplace in her living room. Six twenty-five. Five minutes if he was on time.

Thanks to Annie, the entire meal was ready. Nothing to do there. She did another recheck of her makeup, glanced again at her sheer-stockinged legs to make sure there were no runs and brushed at the skirt of her black dress with the back of her hand.

A car slowed on the street outside her house, turned into the drive with a recognizable rumble, lights piercing the living room window before flicking off.

He was here! Clarice's stomach dropped twenty stories. It seemed like two hours before she heard footsteps on the walk outside, and then the doorbell rang.

She counted to ten—*don't look too anxious, Clarice!*—then went to open it. All the cliché's applied to the man standing on her doorstep. He had on casual clothes, white shirt and jeans, a three-button blazer, and he looked good enough to devour.

''Hi,'' he said, holding up a bottle of red wine.

''Come in,'' she said, waving him inside with one hand, taking the wine with the other. ''Thank you. You didn't have to bring anything, though.''

''Hope red was all right.''

''Red is great. We're having steak. Come on in.'' She waved him inside, beckoning for him to follow her through to the kitchen.

''Nice house,'' he said.

''Thanks. I like it. It's not huge, but I'm gone a lot and don't really need extra space to take care of.''

She opened a drawer, rummaged around for a corkscrew and held it out to him. ''Do you mind opening the wine?''

''No,'' he said and made short work of it while she pulled two glasses from the cupboard above the sink.

"I was surprised to see you in church this morning."

"Figured it would do me good."

"Did it?" she asked, punctuating the question with her most flirtatious smile.

"It certainly didn't hurt," he said, the smile he gave her back falling way short of the response she'd hoped for. Hmm. Too much? Maybe subtle was more appropriate, which wasn't going to be easy. She didn't do subtle. Annie did subtle.

The point didn't pass without a pinprick and a flash of the scene in her sister's kitchen the night of Tommy's birthday party. The look she'd seen on Jack's face then was the one she wanted to see now. Only directed at her.

She led the conversation in a general direction: tell me about your work, what sports do you like. A half hour or so later, she'd employed every Carnegie conversational tactic she knew. But Jack, unlike most men she'd known, had a way of turning a question around so that she ended up doing the talking. "So where did you and Annie grow up?" he asked before she could think of another Carnegie-approved question.

"All over the place," she said, hitching a thumb over her shoulder at the grill visible through the sliding glass door at the back of the kitchen. "Let me just throw these steaks on."

"Can I do that?"

"Got it under control," she said.

He got up from the bar stool and reached for the platter where the two steaks had been marinating. "At least let me carry this."

Clarice smiled. "Thanks."

Outside, she lifted the grill lid, turned on the gas and then forked the steaks onto the rack and closed it again.

"How do you like yours?" she asked.

"Medium well."

"Me, too," she said. Good sign. Anything they had in common was a plus.

They went back inside.

"So what was it like, growing up all over the place?" he asked.

"Daddy never gave up believing the next town would be where he hit it rich. Annie and I never had time at any of our schools to make a best friend. Our houses were always rented, usually with someone else's belongings still scattered in closets and drawers. I didn't mind it so much. But Annie hated it. She always wanted to live in one place, have the same best friend, ride the same school bus every day. One year we had just moved again, I think it was somewhere in Tennessee, right before school started, and Annie actually held a strike in our front yard. Made signs and everything. She didn't want to go to a new school. Of course, being her sister, I was required to participate. Daddy was less than pleased to come home and find his two daughters had formed a union against him."

Jack smiled. And this time it was a real smile. "That must have been hard, starting all over with every new place."

"More so for Annie than me. She was shy to the point of being sick to her stomach the first day of school. I was more the type to go through the front doors both barrels blasting. Which made it easier, no doubt. My skin had gotten thick early on, and if anyone wanted to pick on Annie, they had to come through me first."

"Then she was lucky to have you," Jack said.

"We were lucky to have each other," Clarice said. "We've always been close, except for the first couple years after she married J.D. He didn't like the fact that we were more than sisters."

"Why?" Jack asked.

"Oh, I guess because he knew I had him nailed from the beginning. Annie met J.D. her senior year in high school. He was in town with some minor-league team he was playing on. I was in college and not coming home too much. No one like J.D. had ever paid attention to Annie before, and he pretty much swept her off her feet. He sold her the whole batch of goods about why they should go ahead and get married. Anyway, they did, and I can't say it was the wrong thing, because Tommy wouldn't be here if they hadn't, but I know Annie put her own goals on the back burner so J.D. could chase his dream."

"Playing ball?"

Clarice nodded. "And I can say without hesitation

that she was a big part of the reason he was able to get there. J.D. had talent, no doubt, but he didn't make any money for a long time, and she supported them, really tried to make the marriage work. Which was like trying to push a wheelbarrow full of cement up Mount Everest. And when it came time for the divorce settlement, he somehow managed to make it seem as if Annie had been the one riding on his coattails all along.''

"Was it a bitter divorce?" Jack asked, arms folded across his chest.

"Not on Annie's part. It should have been. No, it was just a case of J.D. thinking of what he always thinks about. His own self-interest.''

"Sounds like you were the bitter one.''

Clarice smiled. "The big sister in me, I guess.''

"That's admirable.''

"Thank you.'' Not exactly the type of positive feedback she was hoping to incite, but hey, it was a start. "Oooh, I better check those steaks.''

"Let me,'' Jack said.

She handed him a fork and knife. He went outside, raised the lid and cut into the center of both pieces. He nodded, and she pulled a platter from the cabinet, passing it to him through the sliding glass doors.

"Smells good,'' he said.

"Great. If you'll pull them off the grill, I'll get everything else ready.''

They ate at Clarice's small dining-room table. Halfway through the meal, guilt-laden by the number of

thank-you's she'd proffered in response to Jack's sin-
cere-sounding compliments, she fessed up and ad-
mitted Annie was the talent behind the meal.

"She's the cook in the family," Clarice said. "I
have pretty much zero talent. Luckily, she enjoys
sharing her skill."

He smiled at that. "That chocolate cake she made
the other night was pretty unbelievable."

"My mom had this old southern cookbook, and for
some reason, Annie loved it. When she was about
thirteen, she started making stuff out of that book. I
think she tried everything in it. Anyway, I thought it
was kind of weird for someone her age to be so into
cooking when I was into begging Mom to let me start
dating and all that stuff. But looking back on it, I
think it was Annie's way of setting down roots. She's
been trying to do that her whole life."

Clarice glanced up just then and caught the look
on Jack's face. And she knew in one of those light-
bulb moments that it wasn't for her. Where this man
was concerned, it was never going to be for her.

AT JUST AFTER MIDNIGHT, Jack sat at the kitchen table
with a batch of C.M. files spread out around him. Pete
had called around eleven, and they'd talked for nearly
an hour, sorting through some business details on
which they'd both needed to state an opinion.

"So when are you heading back?" Pete had asked
when they'd finished with the business stuff. Jack had
surprised himself with his own inability to answer the

question. The trip back to Macon's Point was not following the road map he had envisioned when he'd arrived here.

He picked up one of the files, flipped through it again. He'd run across another piece of interesting information since yesterday. Three of C.M.'s best customers in North Carolina were no longer buying. Earlier that day, he'd made some phone calls and spoken to an irate owner who was happy to tell Jack why his store no longer bought C.M. product. He'd seen the same furniture at local flea markets for half of what he'd paid for it at wholesale.

A couple more calls had gotten him in touch with one of the flea market vendors. Jack had said he was a builder and needed a large amount of product for a series of spec houses he was furnishing. The vendor had assured him it wouldn't be a problem. He had two warehouses of product to choose from. Jack agreed to meet him tomorrow at five o'clock. The man had then given him the addresses to the warehouses. Jack planned to drive down in the morning and take a look around himself.

He stretched his legs out in front of him now, dropped his head back against the chair and stared at the ceiling, conscience stinging. He never should have gone over to Clarice's tonight.

What had he been thinking? That having dinner with Clarice would get his mind off Annie?

Boy, had that backfired.

Annie.

If he'd learned anything tonight, it was that she did not need another guy in her life for whom commitment wasn't in the cards. He didn't like the idea of being paired up with her ex-husband in a comparison contest. But he'd messed up one woman's life by trying to do the exact thing he'd always said he'd never do. By denying what he'd known deep inside was true. Because if a man just didn't believe in something, how could he ever follow it through?

And Jack did not believe that the love a man and woman might start out with would last. He just didn't. He'd seen proof of it in his father's ability to let another woman in his life so quickly. And, too, in the fact that three-fourths of the weddings where he'd been asked to be a groomsman since college had already ended in divorce.

Annie was the kind of woman who did believe in the lasting variety. Who would keep looking for it until she found it. He did not need a flashing neon sign to tell him that; the very way she lived her life gave it perfect illustration.

And he hoped that she did find it.

He wasn't a man who could give that to her, but in the short time he was here, did that mean they couldn't be friends?

ANNIE LAY AWAKE, staring at the ceiling.

She glanced at her alarm clock. Twelve-thirty.

Strange that Clarice hadn't called yet.

She always called after a first date to report initial impressions to Annie and get her read on them.

Ah, Annie, maybe she hasn't called because the date's not over yet.

That realization came at her like a blast of arctic air.

She fish-flopped onto her side and gave her pillow a quick jab it did not deserve.

Go to sleep, Annie. Just go to sleep.

CHAPTER TEN

SHE WAS ON HER WAY out the door to take Tommy to school the next morning when the phone rang. Certain it would be Clarice, Annie picked it up and said, "Hey. Can I call you back from the car?"

"Ah, sure," came a surprised male voice. Jack Corbin's surprised male voice.

Annie froze where she stood. "Jack. I'm sorry. I was sure you were Clarice."

"No problem. I've come across an interesting lead. I thought I'd drive down to North Carolina and check it out. I could use someone to ride shotgun."

"Today?"

"Short notice, I know, but yeah. I'd planned to leave pretty much right away."

Annie's thoughts went in a zillion directions. This, she had not expected. But she'd offered her help in getting to the bottom of anything that might alter the future of Corbin Manufacturing. The fact that she'd spent the night dreaming about his wedding to Clarice shouldn't affect that. "Um, sure. I'd be happy to come along. I was just taking Tommy to school. How long do you think we'll be gone?"

"Maybe early evening?"

"I'll need to check with Mrs. Parker then and make sure she can pick up Tommy. If I don't call you back, that means everything is all right."

"Okay. I'll meet you in your office parking lot. Thirty minutes?"

"See you then."

Annie hung up and dialed Mrs. Parker's number. The older woman assured her it would be no problem for her to fetch Tommy after school. Annie thanked her, then hurried out the front door to where Tommy was already waiting in the Tahoe. Funny thing, too, she felt as though she'd been pumped full of helium, her feet not even touching the ground.

ON THE WAY to Tommy's school, Annie called the office and left a message for Peggy, her receptionist, that she wouldn't be in today. No sooner had she put the phone down than it rang again.

"Morning," Clarice said. "You taking Tommy?"

"Uh-huh," Annie said, starting to tell her about her change in plans for the day, then deciding to ask about Clarice's date first. "So tell me. How did it go?"

"Pretty good, I think. The meal was a hit."

"Good."

"You know men, though. Never can tell what they're thinking."

"I thought you might call last night."

"It was kinda late. Didn't want to wake you."

Clarice always called Annie after dates. Always.

The fact that she hadn't this time meant something. What, though?

Should she tell her about going with Jack today?

She started to, then stopped. What was the point? Annie had no intention of intruding on what she now considered her sister's territory.

So why aren't you telling her then?

Because she might read something into it that wasn't there.

They chit-chatted for another minute or two and then hung up, Annie wondering at her sister's reluctance to go into the specifics of her date. Her normal pattern was to give Annie such a clear picture of events that she might have been there herself.

So what about her own normal pattern? *You never keep things from Clarice!* Unease swam through her. She should have told Clarice about today. Gotten it out in the open so that it wasn't any big deal. Or maybe she should just call Jack back and tell him she couldn't go.

Not professional.

On the assumption that his asking her had been nothing more than a continuation of Saturday's efforts—and that was what she assumed—how could she back out now?

She would call Clarice as soon as they got back, explain how ridiculous she'd been in not telling her, and that would be that.

She did not like being off-kilter with her sister. Clarice meant the world to her, and she would never do anything to hurt her. Men might come and go for both of them, but sisters were forever.

CLARICE HAD JUST SAT down at her desk with a cup of coffee and a story to edit when Tim Filmore swaggered up looking as if he had a secret to sell.

Clarice raised an eyebrow. "Don't you have some stories to write, Tim?"

"How about this for one? Mayor seen leaving town with playboy factory owner."

The words delivered the blow of a two-by-four. "Perfect if you want to go work for the National Tell-All," she managed to answer.

"Probably pay better," he muttered, taking his leave.

"Probably would!" she called out after him, repressing the urge to add she'd be glad to send them his résumé.

Awful thought number one followed: she was in the same boat with Tim. They were both jealous! Awful thought number two: she'd talked to Annie less than an hour ago. Why hadn't she said anything about going somewhere with Jack?

The answer was so obvious it hurt. She hadn't wanted Clarice to know. So why? Because she hadn't wanted her to think it was something it wasn't? Or because it really was?

DAMN IT ALL to hell. J.D. thumped the steering wheel of his red Ferarri with the heel of his right hand. He hated L.A. traffic. He'd been out here a little over a year now, and he'd spent half that time sitting on one or the other of the city's freeways.

Didn't these people mind spending their lives lined up like ants waiting for a picnic? He threw a glance over his shoulder at the three lanes of cars beside him even though it was barely six o'clock in the morning. Nine out of ten drivers had a cell phone stuck to their ear.

A bad mood had hung over him like a stalled thunderstorm all morning. Ever since he'd picked up his mail and found a copy of the *Langor County Times* with a picture of his wife on the front page all cozied up with that born-with-a-silver-spoon-in-his-mouth Jack Corbin. They were at some sort of picnic at Corbin's factory—the one he was apparently closing down.

And the kicker?

There was Tommy looking up at Corbin like he was his father or something!

Damn if he was going to put up with another man making his son forget all about him.

From the corner of his eye, he spotted a blonde in a black BMW giving him a Hey-baby stare. Chicks. This place was overrun with them. A guy could almost get his fill. And maybe he finally had. Cassie was about to drive him crazy. Certifiable.

He was getting sick of her near-daily manicure appointments and root touch-up sessions. And all she ever wanted to do was go out. This party or that club until J.D. forgot what it was like to actually eat dinner at home.

More than once in the last few days, he'd caught himself thinking about Annie and how their house had felt like a home. The house he shared with Cassie felt like a showroom where people only pretended to live. It left him with this gnawing emptiness inside that no matter how much he tried to ignore, never went away.

So maybe he'd liked the fast lane a little more than Annie had, but why couldn't two people find something close to common ground? Some happy medium that worked for them both. Why couldn't that be possible?

It could be. He was sure of it.

But J.D. had known Annie long enough to know there was only one way he would ever get her back.

He pulled his own cell phone from his shirt pocket, hit the directory button, scrolled down until he found the name he was searching for and pushed send.

Four rings. "Russell, Wade."

"Mike? It's J.D. What're you doing answering your own phone?"

"The receptionist is on a coffee run. Didn't think we'd ever hear from you again since you moved West on us." Mike Russell had played high school football with J.D., and the two of them had kept in touch over the years. During his short return to Macon's Point, they'd gotten together for pizza and beer a few times. Mike had handled his divorce from Annie so he knew the nuts and bolts of the marriage's demise. He was a sharp guy, an Ivy League attorney who likely could have made an enviable career for himself in some big city, but had opted for moving back to his hometown. Go figure.

"So how is life in the world of make-believe?"

"Pretty good," J.D. said.

"Been seeing you on TV. Things must be going well."

"Can't complain. You seen Annie lately?"

"Yeah. Saturday night, as a matter of fact. Out at Lugar's."

"Was Tommy with her?"

"Ah, no," Mike said.

J.D. thought about Corbin. His face got hot. "She on a date?"

"I don't know. Kinda looked like it."

"Who with?"

"Jack Corbin. He's about to close down the family business. Apparently, Annie's been trying to change his mind. Maybe she was just trying a new persuasion tactic. Looked like it might be working." Mike laughed.

"Is that right?" J.D.'s voice was cool. The mental image of that needled at him. Corbin had been a couple years behind J.D. and Mike in school. Smart as hell if he remembered right. Seems like he'd broken a couple track records at that fancy private school he'd gone to. And his family business had been the largest employer in town. J.D.'s father had actually worked there for a while.

"Probably wasn't what it looked like," Mike amended, sounding uncomfortable.

"Yeah," J.D. said while something that felt remarkably like jealousy lit up low inside him.

"So what's up, J.D.?"

The line of traffic J.D. was snagged in moved forward a few feet. He shifted into first and revved the Ferrari engine. "I want full custody of my son. Tell me what I need to do to get it."

NEITHER ANNIE NOR Jack said much the first twenty miles or so out of town. Annie felt guilty for not telling Clarice where she was going. What if she saw them? What would she think? *She wouldn't have thought anything if you'd been up-front with her about the whole thing.* As soon as they got back. As soon as they got back.

"So how was last night?" she finally found the voice to ask, aiming for casual.

"Nice," Jack said. "Food was good."

Annie glanced down quickly. "Good."

"Clarice told me you were the chef."

"Oh. Well, she—"

"—told me how you started cooking when you were thirteen. No wonder you're so good at it."

"I—thank you." Flustered, Annie didn't know what else to say. At the moment, she felt like a very bad, very disloyal sister.

A few seconds of silence ticked by. "Annie?"

She looked at him, something in his tone making her heart thump. "What?"

"I'm not exactly sure why I'm telling you this, but I'm not interested in Clarice in that way. She seems like a great person, but—"

"I don't think we should be talking about this," Annie said, the words coming out in a torrent. "I mean, she's my sister and—"

"I know. A good one, it seems."

"Yes. She is."

Confusion settled over Annie like thick fog, blocking out all sense of direction. The safest spot seemed to be keeping her feet planted right where they were. A move in either direction might mean a fall from a really steep place.

They drove on a few miles, then merged onto 220 South. "This may end up being nothing more than a wild-goose chase," Jack said in an obvious change of subject. "I hope it isn't a waste of your day."

"So what's the lead?"

"Flea markets selling product that looks just like C.M. product."

"And you think there might be a connection between that and the missing inventory."

A horse farm lay ahead on their right. Two youngsters romped across one of the fields in what looked like a game of tag. Annie pointed at them. "Is there anything more beautiful than that?"

"My father was always crazy about them. I think out of all this mess, the thing I'm most torn about is

what to do with his two old Percherons. They're an-
cient, and they've lived at Glenn Hall all their lives.''

"Who's been taking care of them?''

"Essie's niece comes by twice a day to feed
them.''

"Will you sell them?''

"Can't stand the thought of it, but I don't know
what other choice I have.''

Annie pictured the two old horses she'd spotted in
the field near Jack's house when she and Clarice had
gone out to see him. Sympathy tugged at her heart.
What an awful decision to have to make. And yet the
very fact that he was torturing himself with it gave
further indication of his nonpermanent status in Macon's Point. Not that she had questioned it.

"You know the way you talk about your dad
doesn't sound like the two of you didn't get along.''

"I loved who he was then. Just not who he became.'' Something on his face snapped closed. Annie
saw it clearly. A window through which she had seen
a boy's adoration of his father dropping shut.

Part of her wanted to pursue it. But she quelled the
urge. That was personal. This trip was not personal.
She did not need to know anything else personal
about him.

The drive to Kernersville was close to two hours.
They hit I-40 just before Greensboro and followed it
another forty-five minutes or so. Conversation between the two of them was sporadic and a little awkward. Something was different this morning. Some

walls in place that hadn't been there before. A distance that felt amplified by Annie's guilty conscience.

Jack reached for a piece of paper on top of the dash and handed it to her. "Would you mind reading those directions for me? I looked before we left, but I don't want to waste time getting us lost."

"Exit 208," Annie said. "Then right on Highway 57. Two miles on left."

"Thanks," Jack said.

The exit came up in just a couple of minutes. They followed the directions to a warehouse.

Jack turned in, stopped in front of a loading door.

They got out, walked to the door. Jack glanced over his shoulder, then tugged on the handle at the bottom of the door. He pulled on it harder. It gave, leaving a crack a couple of inches high at the bottom.

"Would you grab that flashlight out of the side pocket on my door, Annie? I don't want to let this drop in case it won't come up again."

"Sure," she said, jogging over to get it.

"Okay, if you don't want to do this, just say," he said.

"What?" She did a poor job of hiding her skepticism.

"While I hold the door, could you shine the light under? See if you see anything?"

Annie glanced up at the No Trespassing sign centered in clear view on the door. Her stomach dropped a little. "You are planning on bailing me out if we get caught, right?"

"Absolutely," he said, smiling for the first time that morning.

He let go of the door, stuck out a hand and helped her up onto the concrete platform. She lost her balance a little and teetered forward into him. Looking up she found his gaze on her, something unreadable in it. The moment held as if someone had freeze-framed them. Annie felt overheated, as if she'd just run several miles past her level of endurance.

Surely, she had never been this aware of a man. All the clichés applied, and she understood then their origin. Because she really did have sweaty palms, and breathing suddenly required concentrated effort. Hard to believe so much could be said in the span of a few seconds, but if body language could be heard out loud, theirs would have sounded like a football stadium after a winning touchdown.

They both jerked into action at the same moment, he giving the door another heft, she flicking on the flashlight and squatting down on the concrete. "That's not going to work." She stretched out on her stomach facedown. "I'm going to call in favors for this one."

"The view from up here just improved."

Annie looked up quickly, and caught the smile on his far too good-looking face. Was he flirting with her? She felt a blush start at her toes, leap its way straight up to her neck. She ducked her head back down and peered under the bottom of the door. If, big if, that remark had been flirtatious, she had no idea what to do with it. Tim's flirting, she knew what to do with. This, she did not. Anyway, she was wrong. Surely.

"What do you see?" Was it her imagination or did his voice sound different? A little hoarse?

"Just a second." She focused on a shadowed object just inside the door and gave her vision a few moments to adjust. "Looks like a sofa. And a bunch of other furniture. Wood pieces. Hutches and stuff."

"See any tags on anything?"

She flicked the light around, spotted a yellow sticker on one of the pieces. "Corbin Manufacturing," she said.

"So it's ours."

Annie struggled up as gracefully as a prone woman on concrete can. Jack offered her a hand, but she said, "Got it, thanks." Then felt a little silly at the look of surprise on his face. *He was just being polite, Annie.* Fair enough, but she was the one whose pulse went off like a rocket every time he touched her. Better just to avoid that altogether.

"What are you thinking?" she asked.

"That we need to get in this building."

"As in breaking and entering?"

"Well, we'd rather not call it that. Let's walk around, see what we see."

Annie set off after him, at a trot really—heavens, he had a long stride! "Jack, we can't do this. What if someone comes?"

"We'll say we're with the exterminating company. Someone reported bugs here?"

Annie laughed. "My exterminator drives a brown Volkswagen with a big yellow insect on top. You don't look anything like him."

"Glad to hear it. Come on," he waved for her to follow, "where's your sense of adventure?"

"I didn't know potential felons called themselves adventurers."

"Some of us do."

Annie followed behind him, smiling in spite of herself. This was not how she'd imagined her day turning out when she'd gotten up this morning.

They traipsed one short side of the building. Jack headed for the regular-size door at the far corner. Gave it a tug. No luck. Annie breathed a sigh of relief.

"Let's try the other side," Jack said.

"Wait," she said, setting off after him. "There really has to be some other way to do this."

But Jack waded on through the tall grass.

This side of the building backed up to a strip of woods, dense white pines that thinned the sunlight, but made Annie feel a little better about the two of them not being spotted. Safe for the moment, anyway.

They came to another door, this one halfway down the long side of the metal building. Jack stopped in front of it, reached in his back pocket and pulled out his wallet. He fished out a credit card, then dropped down onto one knee in front of the lock.

"You aren't really going to open that door with a credit card, are you?"

"Thought I'd give it a try."

"Jack!"

"There's no one around."

"There might be an alarm system."

"Can you run in those shoes?"

Annie looked down at the less-than-practical two-inch heels she'd slipped on that morning on the way out the door.

"If it goes off, leave the shoes and follow me," he said.

"You're serious, aren't you?"

"We came all this way. I'd like to leave knowing more than I did when I got here."

What in the world did a practical-minded woman like her say to a man intent on breaking into a warehouse?

It was possible, granted, that getting inside would lead him to something that might alter the future of C.M. Seemed overly optimistic, but wasn't that the very thing she'd been fighting for these past few weeks?

"Why don't I run back and take a look at the parking lot? Make sure no one's pulled up."

"Good idea," Jack said without looking up. "In fact, why don't you just stay up there and keep a lookout? Yell if you see anyone."

"You look way too good at that," Annie said,

shaking her head. "I don't even want to know how you came by that particular talent."

"Okay. So I won't tell you."

Annie smiled again in spite of herself, then jogged back the way they'd come, wishing for her very comfortable Nike running shoes. Back at the front corner of the building, she tucked herself beside the gutter spout, glad for its partial concealment, then took a quick peak at the parking lot.

Still empty except for Jack's Porsche. Whew. Sleuthing was definitely not for her. Her palms were sweaty, and her knees felt like the cartilage had been replaced with Jell-O.

She sent a glance back at the door. Jack was nowhere in sight. He'd gotten in! Adrenaline hit her in the center of her chest, spread out to fingers and toes. She glanced at her watch. Five minutes. She would give him five minutes.

Then what?

She couldn't exactly leave.

Oh, hurry, Jack! Just hurry!

The next few minutes passed like the pouring of nearly-set concrete. *Stay calm, Annie.* Just a little longer, and surely he'll be done.

She glanced at her watch 354 times—or so it seemed, anyway. Fifteen minutes, and still no sign of him! Where was he?

Another five ticked by. Okay, she was going after him. Something was obviously wrong.

She started back through the tall grass but thought

she heard something and stopped. The sound was un-mistakable. Tires crunching on gravel.

Annie whipped around, ran back to the front corner of the building, took a quick peek around the side, praying she wouldn't be seen.

Someone had just pulled up beside the Porsche. A man in some kind of uniform. A security guard. He got out, circled the car, looking inside.

Annie tore off through the grass again, quelling the urge to yell for Jack. He'd left the door open. She slipped inside. The place was totally dark except for the dim light slanting through two skylights in the ceiling.

"Jack!" Her hushed voice sounded like a whisper in the enormous warehouse. She'd just have to risk it. She had to get his attention. "Jack!" she called out again, louder this time.

"Over here."

"There's someone here! A security guard, I think. He's outside looking at the car."

Lights flooded the warehouse, sudden, blinding. Annie saw spots.

"Is somebody in here?" came a voice from the front of the building.

Fear slashed through her. They were caught! Oh good heavens, they were caught!

And then Jack was beside her, grabbing her hand, a finger to his lips indicating for her to be quiet. He took her hand and pulled her along toward the door they'd come in through. Good thing, too, because she couldn't have moved herself from that spot had her life depended on it.

Which it probably did.

They slipped through the door, Jack reaching back to let it click quietly closed behind them. And then they were running back through the grass, faster than Annie had ever run in her life—heels be damned! Amazing what they could do when summoned.

Visions of the security guard coming out the door behind them, gun in hand, had her picking up the pace. Hardly the time to be noticing such a thing, but Jack's hand felt strong and good holding onto hers. And it was kind of nice the way he squeezed hers between his as if he'd never let go.

A few seconds, and they were back in the parking lot. "Mind if I don't get your door this time?"

"You're forgiven this once," Annie said, running around the Porsche and jumping inside.

Jack turned the key, and for one heartstopping instant, Annie thought it wasn't going to start. It did, and she slid down in the seat. "I'll never be bad again. I'll never be bad again."

Jack looked over at her and laughed.

Laughed!

"Tell me what you could possibly find funny about this," she said as he gunned the Porsche out of the parking lot, gravel and dust whirling up behind them.

"It's not," he said, straightening his expression into seriousness. "You're right. Nothing humorous about it."

Annie shot a glance back at the building. "I don't see him."

At the company entrance, Jack barely slowed down, sending a quick look both ways before shooting back onto the highway and flooring the car.

"Okay, so these cars do have a selling point,' she said, flattened against her seat.

"If you need to get there fast—"

"I'm sure a big slice of their market pie must be the criminal element."

Jack laughed again, sinking the gearshift into fifth, and it felt as if they were flying. A mile or two down the road, he let up, and the car reluctantly settled into a speed that was in agreement with the law.

"Don't think I'm not totally disgusted with you," she said, arms folded across her chest.

"You probably don't want to know what I found out then?" The question held a teasing note.

"What?" So much for cool indifference.

"There's a good bit of stuff in there that still has C.M. tags on it. But there's a lot more, things recognizably part of the line, that have been retagged under another manufacturer's name."

Annie frowned. "Why?"

"That's the question."

"You think it's stolen?"

"Kinda looking that way. But the trick is going to be figuring out by whom and why."

"Would it have to be someone working inside C.M?"

"That would make the most sense. This address is listed as belonging to a legitimate customer, and it's obviously not what it was supposed to be."

"So maybe someone is reselling the product?"

"That's what I'm thinking."

Annie's stomach dropped. She felt suddenly sick. "Who would do something like that?"

"I don't know. Maybe someone with a grudge against the company or just plain old-fashioned greed."

"Embezzling but with actual product instead of cash."

"Yeah."

"So one person or maybe a few are responsible for bleeding the company dry?"

"Could be," Jack said.

"And yet the whole town is blaming you for it?"

"I'm not worried about that, Annie. It doesn't matter what everyone thinks about me."

"It does," she said, sensing in the evenness of his tone that it really did matter to him. "Of course it does. And especially when it's not true."

He looked at her, taking his gaze from the road for just a moment, but it was long enough for Annie to catch a glimpse of something that looked like vulnerability there. He did care. She knew it somehow. Awareness of that stirred something inside her. Unexpected, but deep and real.

Annie...you are treading in dangerous waters.

No doubt.

"So what are you going to do next?" She sat straighter in the seat, put her gaze on the countryside rolling by her window and her thoughts on what they'd just discovered.

He reached for a piece of paper on the dash. Handed it to her and said, "This was the other place I wanted to check out. Shouldn't be more than thirty minutes from here."

"Are you planning to use your credit card there, too?"

"We'll stick to legal looking around at this one."

"You're sure?"

He held up two fingers. "Scout's honor."

"And you really were one?"

"Honest."

CHAPTER ELEVEN

THIRTY MINUTES LATER, they pulled into the parking lot of another building that looked remarkably like the one they'd been in earlier.

Jack pulled into a parking space and left the engine running. "You wait here. I'll be right back."

"You're not going in there, are you?"

"Just a quick look around the building."

"I've heard that one before."

Jack smiled. "Used up all my credibility this morning, I take it?"

"Approaching. What if someone comes?"

"Tell them I went in search of a little boys' room," he said, grinning, expecting her cheeks to go red and watching it happen. It hit him then that he'd never met a woman who looked so good when she was blushing. Not sure what to do with that thought, he took off, heading to the back of the building.

Halfway down the back was a door with a window on each side. He looked through the glass, waiting for his eyes to adjust. Yep. C.M. furniture. Rows and rows of it. He really needed to go inside, but he'd promised Annie, and granted they'd pushed their luck at the other place.

He had enough to go on for now, anyway.

He headed back to the car. Rounded the front of the building to see Annie standing outside of the Porsche talking to someone in what looked like a navy blue security guard uniform.

She looked over her shoulder just then and spotted him. "Oh, here's my husband, sir. Jack, I was just telling the officer about your bladder problem."

Jack's eyebrows shot skyward. What?

Annie was still talking. "You know, it's really a horrible thing, Officer. And for such a young man, too. Makes traveling take twice as long as it normally would. What with stopping at every other exit off the highway. This time we didn't even make it to the next one. We saw this empty parking lot and wheeled right in here. We certainly never intended to trespass, but when nature calls—"

"All right, ma'am," the flustered-looking officer said, holding up a hand and shooting a look at Jack, who had on his best embarrassed husband face. None of which was an act except for the husband part. "You all get on down the road now."

"Yes, sir," Annie said. "Come on, honey. Let's see if we can cover ten or twenty miles before the next stop."

They got in the car then, both of them straight-faced as he did a calm U-turn in the parking lot and headed back to the main road. The tires had no sooner hit the asphalt of Highway 124 than Annie began laughing.

"I guess that's what's known as a payback?" Jack patted the side of his face where his cheeks were still burning.

"You're—" The laughter had turned into giggles now, and she could barely finish her sentence. "You're embarrassed."

"No, I'm not, really," he began denying it, and then, "Okay, so I'm embarrassed. My bladder problem?"

"Well, I had to come up with something. When I saw him pulling into the parking lot, I nearly had a heart attack."

"And it's believable that a big, strong guy like me has a bladder problem?"

The giggles hit her again then, and she actually bent forward, holding her stomach.

"Oh, my goodness, I'm sorry, I—"

"Quite all right. I'll be looking at an image makeover when we get home."

More giggles, and he thought to himself that it was a really nice thing to make a woman like her laugh that hard.

Finally, she leaned her head back against the seat and sighed. "I was just hoping I could wear him down by talking him to death."

"Looked like it was working."

"I should really be mad at you, you know. I thought we were done for."

"Have to admit I did, too. Nice to have a partner who thinks on her feet," he teased.

"Even when it's at your expense?"

"Even when."

She smiled again, was silent for a moment, and then added, "Kind of odd to have such regular security checks around warehouses, don't you think?"

"Yeah, it does seem a little coincidental."

"For us to have run into both of them, they must get by pretty regularly."

"Must."

"So what are you going to do about all of this?" Annie asked, her tone more somber now.

Jack sighed. "Good question. I guess the first step is to try and figure out if there's anyone whose lifestyle seems to be larger than their income."

"This is terrible," Annie said, sighing. "I just can't imagine who it would be. I know most of the people who work there. I go to church with a lot of them."

"I guess that doesn't always guarantee living right."

"Sadly, no."

Jack glanced at his watch. "It's nearly three o'clock. Are you starving?"

"A little hungry," Annie said.

"The least I can do for the Oscar-winning performance is buy you lunch."

Annie smiled. "The least."

THEY GOT BACK to Macon's Point just before six. Jack pulled into the municipal building parking lot beside Annie's car.

"I think I'll go over to the factory and do a little more digging," he said.

"I wish there were another explanation for what we saw today."

"So do I."

"If you want some help later, let me know. I'll be at home."

"You've gone beyond the call of duty."

"I didn't mind."

He held her gaze for a moment, and Annie was really sorry the day had to end.

"I had fun today, Annie," he said.

"So did I." The admission was out before she'd given it the consideration that might have denied its existence.

They sat there a while longer, as if neither of them knew exactly where to go with the information.

Finally, Annie said, "Well, I'd better go."

"Thanks again for going with me."

"Not a problem." She threw a wave at him as she got into her own car and headed down Main Street.

Amazing how much they'd laughed today.

There was something really nice about the way that felt.

Somewhere along the way, she and J.D. had reached the point where laughter was not a part of their lives. Maybe that should have been her first warning sign that things were headed in a bad direction. But she'd gone along thinking that nobody's life was perfect, and a good wife just tried to make things work.

Today had reminded her how nice it was to have laughter.

She thought about the moments during the day when she had felt Jack's gaze on her. Felt the undercurrent of attraction that she had so far managed to convince herself she must be imagining. She was aware of it. Way down in that place where the usual self-doubts had squelched it numerous times. No way would a man like that be interested in you, Annie. But then she hadn't said interested in. She'd said attracted to.

And that she had seen in his eyes today. Recognized it as the mirror image of her own awareness of him.

She felt the pull of physical desire now, more deeply intense than any she had ever felt. She indulged it for a few moments, dwelling on its possibilities, on what it would be like to kiss him. Just the notion filled her with the kind of jitters more appropriate to a sixteen-year-old girl than a woman who should know better.

It wasn't something she had expected to feel. Nor had wanted to. In recent months, she had finally gotten her life well-oiled enough again that it had a pattern and rhythm that she found comforting. No, she did not have a husband. Or a boyfriend. But she had peace. And self-respect.

So why did it have to be this man? At this time?

Her life did not need this kind of complication. Because she didn't have only herself to think of. There was Clarice. Clarice! Not once during the entire day had she let herself remember that it was her sister who'd had a date with Jack last night. And yet Jack had made it clear that he wasn't interested in Clarice like that. Annie felt at once relieved and traitorous.

Annie was a play-by-the-rules kind of woman. She liked to know what they were right up front and was most comfortable sticking to them. Letting herself admit an attraction to a man to whom her sister had already staked a verbal claim did not come anywhere near playing by the rules.

Tommy was playing outside in the yard when Annie pulled up to the house a few minutes later.

"Mama!" He came running the second he saw her, and her heart lifted. "You're back!"

"How was school?" She crossed the gravel drive, dropped down and welcomed his tumult into her arms. She hugged him hard for a few moments, then pulled back and ruffled his hair. "I believe you grew today."

Tommy laughed. "You can't grow in a day, Mama."

"Oh. Well, maybe you just look taller."

He took her hand, led her up the walkway to the side door off the kitchen, telling her what happened at school as they went.

Mrs. Parker came to the door, swung it open for them and smiled a greeting.

"Hope I haven't held you up, Mrs. Parker."

"Not at all," she said, stepping back so they could all file into the house. "Tommy's had his dinner. I made us some chicken and dumplings. Hope that was all right."

"Of course," Annie said, hanging her coat in the mudroom.

"We saved you a plate."

"Thank you."

They went into the kitchen where Mrs. Parker reached for a bowl on the counter and put it away. "I'll be going then. Oh, let's see, where did I put that note? There it is." She picked up a piece of paper off the island and handed it to Annie. "Michael Russell called for you. Just after four. He asked if you could call him as soon as you have a chance. Said he would be working late at the office tonight."

Annie's stomach dropped. What in the world could that be about? Mike had been J.D.'s attorney in their divorce. He had been reluctant, initially, to get involved. He knew them both. Had eaten dinner at their house. He would have been much happier staying out of it. But J.D. had been persistent, and Mike had given in. To this day, he still had trouble meeting eyes with Annie when they passed on the street. He was a good attorney, and his efforts on J.D.'s part had not contributed to the size of her bank account.

She glanced at the note. Alarm jangled through her.

She neutralized it with a quick, *It's probably nothing, Annie. Don't go making a big deal out of something that isn't.*

But when it came to J.D., Annie had learned to expect the unexpected.

"Are you all right, Annie?"

She looked up to find Mrs. Parker studying her through concerned eyes.

"Oh, yes," she said. "I'm fine. Thank you."

"Well, if you're sure, then I'll be on my way."

Annie thanked the older woman again for picking Tommy up from school. She walked her to the door and watched until she'd gotten in her car and backed out of the driveway. She looked down at the note still clutched between her fingers.

She picked up the phone and punched in the number. A woman answered and said she would check to see if Mike was still in the office.

"Mike Russell," he answered a few moments later.

"Mike. I got your message. What's up?"

"Hey, Annie," Mike said, the seriousness of his voice putting her instantly on guard. "I don't guess there's any reason to beat around the bush. You're not going to like this no matter how I put it. J.D. is filing for custody of Tommy."

Annie's fingers went slack, and she almost dropped the receiver. "What—what did you say?"

"I'm sorry, Annie." An audible sigh echoed across the line. "There's nothing about divorce that's easy.

Seems like it would work out a lot better if people just stayed together.''

Annie laughed. Laughed when her heart felt as if a huge pair of pliers had just yanked it from her chest. ''I assume you mean even when one of the parties doesn't believe in fidelity.''

''Annie, I know none of this is what you wanted, and I hate to drop this on you. But he's serious.''

''This is the most ridiculous thing I've ever heard. He doesn't stand a chance of getting Tommy.''

Silence from the other end.

''Does he?'' she asked, less certain now.

''You'll want to give your attorney a call.''

''Mike—'' She broke off, wanting to say a thousand things at once and knowing, suddenly, that none of them mattered.

''I'm sorry, Annie.''

She put the phone back on its cradle. Emotion stormed through her: disbelief, anger, outrage.

What did J.D. think he was doing? He had ripped their life up, tossed it out the window, taken off for California with his twenty-something bride-to-be, and now he wanted her son out there, too?

Not in this lifetime!

She picked up the phone again, flipped through her Rolodex to J.D.'s L.A. number, punched it in fiercely enough to damage both finger and keypad. Voicemail picked up on the third ring.

''Hello. J.D. and I are out just now—''

Annie cut the message off. She paced the kitchen

floor, then stopped and dropped her forehead onto the heel of one hand. Take a deep breath. This whole thing was nothing but ludicrous. There was no way J.D. could ever get Tommy.

Fear knifed through her with a question she'd yet to consider. Given the choice, would Tommy want to live with his father? What if he did?

Clarice. Call Clarice. She'll put the whole thing in perspective. Where J.D. was concerned, she always did.

CLARICE WAS IN THE KITCHEN clearing out the last of the dishes in the dishwasher when the phone rang.

Just the sound of it cranked the intensity of her five-alarm headache. It had been that kind of day.

She picked up the cordless from the countertop, glanced at the number on caller ID.

Annie.

Clarice chewed her lower lip, emotions she was not proud of bubbling inside her.

And for the first time in her life, she didn't take her sister's call.

ESSIE WAS STILL at the house when Jack got home after dropping Annie off. From the back door, he heard the clatter of pots and pans and followed it to the kitchen. She was standing on a ladder, wiping out one of the high-up cabinets.

"Give you a hand with that?"

She turned with a start, hand to her chest. "Land

sakes! Do you want to be responsible for making an old woman fall off her ladder?''

Jack laughed. ''You're too agile for that.''

She smiled. ''I was just cleaning up a bit. You had dinner?''

''Late lunch.''

''Left you something in the oven. If you get hungry later, it'll be there.''

''Thank you, Es. You're spoiling me, though.''

''Doesn't hurt once in a while. I guess with the kind of work you do, you don't get many home-cooked meals.''

''That's a fact,'' he said, opening the refrigerator and pulling out the pitcher of iced tea she made fresh every day. And there in the kitchen where he'd grown up, where he'd enjoyed countless home-cooked meals, something hit him solidly between the ribs. An absolutely recognizable feeling that he could stay. That he didn't have to go back to his other life. A life that kept him on the road all the time, that before now had seemed like a perfectly good life.

He frowned at the intensity of the feeling, wondered at its immediate depth and breadth as if it had been forming without his awareness.

Essie got down from the ladder and closed the cabinet door. ''Your father would be proud of what you're doing.''

Jack set down the pitcher, his expression hardening. ''I didn't start this for him.''

She looked at him for a long moment, silent. ''You

know, son, I'm afraid you're going to live the rest of your life with all that anger as your compass, and that would be a shame. A real shame.''

She left the kitchen then, her disappointment in him still hanging in the air.

He started to call her back, but caught himself. What was the point? He did not expect her to understand. Essie had loved Jack's father the way she would have a brother. Her loyalty to him was fierce. The way Jack saw it, Essie would have forgiven his father anything. Had forgiven him anything.

''You never knew how I came to work here, did you?''

He looked up. Essie had come back and stood in the kitchen doorway now, her usually smiling face somber. He shook his head. She wrung the bottom of the apron tied to her waist between her hands. ''I got married when I was sixteen. We were poor, and this fella came along that just seemed like he was going to fix everything, for me and my family. I suspect they didn't mind getting rid of me. I had eight brothers and sisters, and one more mouth to feed was one more mouth to feed. At first, everything was better than I ever imagined, which I guess should have been my first warning sign. We'd only been married a month when he hit me the first time.''

Jack frowned. ''Ah, Es.''

She fixed her gaze on her hands as if some part of her had gone back to that place in her memory. ''I was outraged, went home to my family. But they sent me right back. Wives didn't leave their husbands. If things weren't perfect, well not much in life was. A year after we'd gotten married, I'd already been to the emergency room four times. Each one a little worse than the other. To the point I was too embarrassed to drag myself in there again.''

She stopped, still not looking at him. He waited, sensing she needed to finish.

The grandfather clock in the living room struck nine. The kitchen faucet dripped against the stainless-steel sink. ''I had taken a job over at Kinley's as a cashier. Your father used to come in and buy that apple pie ice cream he always liked. One night, I guess I looked a sight because I could see in his eyes, he knew exactly what had happened to me. He took out a card and wrote down his name and your mother's name with a phone number and said if I ever needed any help, all I had to do was call.''

She laughed a little, the tail end of it disappearing into a soft sob. ''Do you know I actually got desperate enough to do just that? There wasn't anybody else willing to help me, so I called one night at work, and he and your mother came and picked me up. They gave me a place to stay and a job, and the two times Joseph showed up to tell me I better get myself back home if I knew what was good for me, your daddy greeted him at the door with a shotgun. He never came back.''

''Essie, I had no idea,'' Jack said, understanding

for the first time in his life the strong ties this woman felt to his family.

"As sure as I'm standing here, I know I wouldn't be alive today if it weren't for your father, Jack. And no, he wasn't a saint. He had weaknesses and flaws just like the rest of us. But he was a good man. And losing your mother nearly killed him. That much I know. What they had was special."

"Then how could he have forgotten about her so soon?"

"Oh, son, he didn't forget. He never forgot. Daphne told me once that she knew Joshua would never love her the way he'd loved your mother. She didn't expect him to. But she helped him through a very bad time, helped him see some light on the other end. He was grateful for that. It's always been my feeling that if he hadn't married Daphne, he probably would have died of heartbreak. People handle things in different ways, son. But we all do what we have to do to get by."

She turned and left the kitchen again then, her shoulders a little hunched as if bearing the weight of all that she had just told him.

Jack stood there, feeling as if everything inside him had shifted, leaving little that was recognizable. For so long, he'd closed his mind to the man he'd once thought his father to be. Evidence of his father's character had been relayed to him more than once since he'd come back to Macon's Point, by Henry Sigmon, the man who'd worked for so long at C.M., and now by Essie, who had been all but a second mother to Jack.

Could she be right? Had Joshua done what he'd had to do to survive losing the love of his life?

The questions needled Jack now with something that felt undeniably like truth at its tip.

He went to the sideboard where his father had once kept his whiskey, found that it was still there. He poured himself a shot of Basil Hayden and took it outside on the back porch where he collapsed into one of the old rockers there. The chair was old and squeaked in fifty different places. The September night air was cool. The moon was just short of full, throwing light across the pasture to the left of the barn and the shadows of Ned and Sam, grazing, the days still warm enough that they spent most of it in the shade of the maple tree in the center of the field.

Jack swigged the bourbon. He'd never been much of a drinker but welcomed the burn down his throat as a change of focus from the other burn centered in his heart. He dropped his head against the back of the rocker. Closed his eyes and concentrated on the squeaking chair. But it failed to drown out the questions surfacing inside him, so he stopped rocking and let himself hear them.

Had he been too hard on his father? Refused to see that maybe his grief had been too much to bear alone?

Had he really loved Jack's mother as Jack had once believed?

Jack had lived his adult life under the premise that

love like that was little more than a fairy tale. Refusing to commit to one woman because commitments did not last, and affirmations of forever love were nothing more than hollow promises. Oh, he'd believed it could last a while. Years, even. But something always came along to change it. Or maybe it was just that people eventually allowed it to be changed.

He thought about the rift between his father and him. Of how it had grown wider with each passing year until mending it seemed an impossible thing. Jack had let his bitterness blind him to anything other than what he'd believed to be true.

He would never have the chance to fix that. The weight of the realization felt enormous to him now. And he realized suddenly that Essie was right. He didn't want to let all the old anger at his father be the compass that determined his future.

Sitting there in the old rocker, he wished he'd found his way to this point a long time ago, that he could have put aside his stubbornness and found a way to talk to his father. That was a regret he would have to live with. And not one he was proud of.

A picture of Annie joined the hum in his head. As she'd looked that afternoon on the drive back, smiling, a little flushed from the craziness of the day.

He could not remember the last time he'd enjoyed a woman's company as he'd enjoyed Annie's today. There was something about being with her that felt natural and easy. One conversation flowed into another. Whether he started it, or she started it, they blended so seamlessly that it seemed as if they had known one another for years.

But then everything about his attraction to Annie was different.

The admission tripped him a little, and he was hit with the sudden sensation of falling, fast and hard.

He took another swig of his whiskey, feeling its rush, and the simultaneous unbalancing of the convictions he'd held onto for so long. It felt as if he had finally reached a place of understanding where his father was concerned. Fortuitous, that on this same day, he should wonder, too, if he had met the woman who could make him believe once and for all that real love was not a fairy tale?

CHAPTER TWELVE

AT EIGHT-FIFTEEN the next morning, Annie was pacing the floor of Eric Bailer's office. He'd handled her divorce from J.D. A soft-spoken man with thinning brown hair, he wasn't the stereotypical nail-'em-to-the-wall divorce attorney. For the most part, he did a lot more considering than talking, the result being that when he did say something, it usually had meaning, and people listened.

He hadn't said a word past hello since Annie had flown into his office and given him a sixty-second rundown of the phone call she'd received from Mike Russell.

Annie had just reached the breaking point when he said, "Hmm. No doubt this isn't a desirable development."

"There's no way he could ever gain full custody, is there?"

"I try to make a practice of never saying never. It's unlikely, true. But he could certainly make your life miserable trying."

Annie wanted to cry. Drop to the floor right there in front of him and wail like a baby. Remorse struck her for the times when she'd felt the inconvenience of being a mother. Like the night she'd had to take Tommy with her to Walker's to meet Jack. No, motherhood wasn't always convenient. But nothing, nothing in her life meant more to her. Tommy was her center, her focus, the rudder that kept her upright. She could no longer even imagine her daily life without him.

J.D. couldn't do this. Not after everything else he'd done.

But then he could. And he would use the same line of logic he'd always used to justify his behavior. He was J. D. McCabe. What more logic did he need?

ANNIE TRIED TO CALL Clarice again as soon as she got back to her office. Where was she? And why wasn't she answering the cell phone she kept with her at all times?

She sat in the chair behind her desk, staring at the cup of coffee she had yet to touch. She felt locked up inside, as if someone had put her in an instant deep freeze.

What was she going to do?

She could not, would not let J.D. take her son away.

HE COULD HAVE dressed it up under a dozen different excuses, but the truth was there was one reason, and only one, that had Jack taking the stairs to Annie's office in the municipal building just before eleven that morning.

He wanted to see her.

He had woken up to that reality and felt it intensify inside him with every hour since.

There was no one at the front desk, so he followed the hallway to her office, stopped in the doorway. She sat behind the desk, profile to him, her gaze on some point outside the window, or much farther away than that judging from the look on her face.

"Annie?"

She looked up, surprise widening her eyes for a moment. "Jack. I'm sorry. I didn't hear you come in."

"No one was out there," he said, hitching a thumb over his shoulder, "so I just—"

"That's fine. Come in," she said, standing.

From ten feet away, he could see the strain on her face, the tension in her shoulders, heard a note in her voice that made it sound like someone else's voice altogether. "Are you all right?"

"Ah, yes. Could I get you something? Coffee?"

"No. I'm fine, thanks."

She stood facing him, palms pressed to the top of her desk as if that were the only thing holding her upright. "So did you find out anything else—"

"What's wrong, Annie?" The question was out on the gut instinct that the devastated look in her eyes meant something.

She all but crumpled before him, like a tent with the pegs suddenly pulled, dissolving onto the chair behind her desk. "I'm sorry, Jack. I'm fairly worthless at everything this morning. I really need to just go home and—''

He was around the desk in less than two seconds, again before giving himself time to consider any of the reasons why it might be a bad idea. He dropped to one knee, turned the swivel chair so they were face-to-face. Up close, her despair was impossible to miss. Her eyes red-rimmed, what makeup she had on streaked and tear-damaged. ''What happened?''

''Something personal.'' She sighed, her gaze on the hands in her lap. ''I'll work through it. I'm just a little blindsided at the moment.''

''I'd like to help, Annie. Let me.''

She lifted her chin then, the look in her eyes so vulnerable and terrified that he had the immediate and overwhelming urge to take her in his arms, wrap her up tight and swear to her that everything was going to be all right. No matter what the problem was.

He put a clamp on that and made himself wait.

''I...J.D.'s lawyer called yesterday. He's filing for custody of Tommy.''

The words hit Jack dead center in the chest. Stunned him to the point that his mind went blank. He finally found voice enough to say, ''No court in its right mind would take Tommy from you.''

She looked up at him, hope flaring in her eyes. And he prayed to God he was right, that his words weren't just platitudes. Annie was a wonderful mother; Tommy was the focus of her life. It was one of the first things he'd realized about her—that love for her son and the pride she took in making a home for him, wanting him to grow up feeling secure and cherished. He knew these things to be true. They were qualities, he realized suddenly, for which he respected her.

"I want to believe that," she said, "but I keep thinking about all the things that could happen, about how much J.D. hates to lose when he decides he wants something—"

"Wouldn't he want what's best for Tommy?"

She sighed again. "J.D. has a way of figuring out what's best for others by first deciding what's best for him."

Jack started to offer an opinion on J.D.'s apparent lack of character, but decided against it, suspecting his reasons were tinted with something else besides amazement at the man's obvious lack of care for the pain he was causing Annie. Now wasn't the time to take a look at those reasons.

"I know what you need," he said, standing and pulling her to her feet in front of him. "A blue plate special. With extra mashed potatoes."

"Oh, I don't think so," she started to protest.

"No arguments," he said, taking her by the hand and leading her out of the office. "Essie used to say people and shirts have two things in common. Starch always improves them."

WALKER'S WAS NEARLY FULL when they got there. Charlotte Turner was working the front. She looked at Jack, then winked at Annie and gave her a thumbs-up. Annie's face went warm. Charlotte had obviously drawn her own conclusions. She put them at one of the last tables left in the back. Despite the numbness settling over her senses, Annie was aware that nearly every person in the place looked up as they threaded their way through the room. She could practically hear their thoughts. Has she changed his mind yet?

They were sitting down with a glass of iced tea in front of them when Jack said, "So what does your lawyer think?"

"That we need to just wait and see exactly what J.D. is asking for."

"Sounds logical."

She nodded. "Except I'm feeling anything but logical right now."

"Annie, you're an incredible mother. Anyone who bothers to look can see that."

They were words she needed to hear just then. Since she'd left her attorney's office earlier that morning, fear had been gaining more and more of a foothold inside her. She reached for the reasoning in his voice like a lifeline.

"It's the scariest thing I've ever imagined. Losing him."

"You won't lose him."

She wished for his certainty, told herself that in all likelihood he was right. But then he didn't know what J.D. could be like when he decided he wanted something.

"Hey, you two."

Annie looked up. Clarice stood beside the table, wearing a smile that fell about as far short of convincing as any she'd ever seen on her. "Clarice," she said. "Did you get my message earlier?"

"Yeah. I just hadn't had a chance to call you back." She looked at Jack, smiled another neutral smile. "Hey, Jack."

"How's it going, Clarice?"

"Good," she said, sounding, Annie thought, brittle around the edges.

"Would you like to join us?" he asked.

"Oh, no," she said. "Don't want to intrude, and anyway, I'm meeting someone."

"Who?" Annie asked.

"Wallace."

"Kingsley?" Annie did a poor job of hiding her shock.

Clarice nodded. "He should be here any minute."

Clarice couldn't stand the man. Called him Wallace-the-thirty-two-arm-octopus. Annie could barely meet eyes with him now and not bubble into laughter. So why was Clarice having lunch with him?

Wallace appeared just then, coming up behind Clarice and putting a proprietary tentacle on her shoulder. "Hey, doll," he said. Annie knew her sister, knew the smile Clarice pasted on her face was fake, that she was forcing herself not to slap his hand away.

"Hi, Wallace. You know Annie. And this is Jack Corbin. Jack, Wallace Kingsley."

Jack stood up, shook the man's hand, which happened to be the one not clamped to Clarice's shoulder. "Good to meet you."

"Corbin. You're the one about to close down the factory, I hear," Wallace said.

"Wallace." Clarice's tone was a verbal swat.

The waitress appeared with their lunch plates.

"Looks good," Clarice said. "We'll leave you to it."

"Call me later?" Annie called out after her sister, who had already turned to leave and answered with a wave.

The waitress placed a plate in front of them both. "Anything else I can get you?" she asked.

"We're good," Jack said.

Annie glanced across the room where Clarice and Wallace had taken a table facing the window. She could see Clarice's hurt in the very set of her shoulders. Knew that she had somehow found out about yesterday and understood the unreturned phone calls. Suddenly, the plate in front of Annie lost all appeal. She glanced at her watch, deep-rooted loyalty for her sister making her say, "Oh, goodness. You know what, I've got to get back to the office. There are about fifteen things I need to get done today before it's time to pick up Tommy."

"Annie, wait—"

She pushed her chair back, reached for the bill the waitress had left on the table. "I'll get this on the way out."

For the rest of the day Clarice was in a stew.

Everyone in the office did their best to avoid her. Question du jour? What is up with her?

True enough, she wasn't going to win any personality awards from her colleagues this afternoon. She'd built herself a fairly high pedestal of indignation. She excused her behavior with her own sense of betrayal. By Annie. That was the part that hurt so much. Her own sister. How could she be so uncaring of Clarice's feelings?

So maybe she could be accused of making assumptions. As mayor, Annie had a role in this whole C.M. business, granted. It could be reasoned that her meetings with Jack were nothing more than strategy sessions or whatever. Reasoned, that was, except for the few seconds when she'd observed the two of them today before they'd ever realized she was in the restaurant.

That look!

A person would have to be a turnip to miss it!

Never in her life had Clarice seen that look on Annie's face before. She was smitten with the man. Smitten!

And it was her guess that he wasn't much better off. She'd felt the force field around that table from twelve feet back.

Served her right, she supposed, for staging that whole thing. From the post office across the street, she'd seen the two of them go into Walker's, and in a moment of desperation—not to mention a momentary loss of good sense—she'd corralled a startled-looking Wallace who'd been coming in the post office into taking her to lunch, a proposition to which he agreed with respect-reducing haste.

"Why, Clarice," he'd said. "I was sure you were blowing me off, ignoring my phone calls after our date a few weeks ago."

She'd intended to call him just as soon as the first-date-hand-swatter he'd inspired her to invent rolled off the assembly lines. "Now, Wallace," she'd said, "don't go imagining things."

If he hadn't been in possession of an ego the size of Colorado, she might have felt guilty. But she couldn't have made a ding in his self-image with a crowbar and a large sledgehammer.

Heaven save her from these duds!

Why was it that she couldn't meet a good man? And why was it that just when she thought she had, Annie had to mess the whole thing up?

ANNIE FUMBLED HER WAY through the next two days, regretful and worried. Regretful that she'd left Walker's the way she had Tuesday. *Professional, Annie!* Worried about what was beginning to feel like a serious rift with Clarice and the nagging concern over J.D.'s latest hijacking of her life.

She had just set Tommy's dinner on the table Thursday night when the phone rang. Maybe it was Clarice finally returning one of the dozen or so messages Annie had been leaving for her.

"Hey, Annie, it's Jack. Is this a bad time?"

"Ah, no." And then, hesitating, "I'm sorry for leaving so fast at lunch Tuesday."

"I was considering changing my aftershave."

"Your aftershave is fine. I just…things are kind of complicated."

"With Clarice?"

Annie hesitated, then sighed. "Yeah."

"I don't want to cause problems for you, Annie."

"You're not. And anyway, let me worry about that."

"And what about J.D.? No chance he's changed his mind?"

"Not that I've heard."

"So I'm thinking you need another outing with Jack Corbin, private eye extraordinaire."

"The kind where I'll worry about getting shot or going to jail?"

"Much tamer than that."

Annie smiled. "So what's the plan?"

JUST OVER AN HOUR LATER, Annie pulled into Jack's driveway and cut the engine of the Tahoe. She sat there for a moment, debating the wisdom of agreeing to meet him tonight. She should make some excuse. The line between her legitimate obligation to help re-route the fate of Corbin Manufacturing and her own attraction to its owner had blurred to the point where she couldn't honestly say which had more weight.

As far as C.M. was concerned, she felt obligated,

and, yes, wanted to help him in any way she could. But on another level, a personal level, she had to be honest with herself. There was an undercurrent of something else pulling them along now. Unspoken, but there. Awareness of one another. The desire to follow it, see where it led. The final destination was without doubt the edge of that cliff she'd been envisioning. But there was a lot of straight road before that point, some sights along the way that Annie yearned to see and had not seen in a very long time. And never with a man like Jack.

Never with a man like Jack.

The front porch light flicked on, and he came out, a jacket over his arm. She got out of the Tahoe. "Hi."

"Hi," he said.

And there was a second, just one, maybe two, when something good settled over them, identifiable to Annie not as a single thing, but a combination of pure physical awareness tempered with a thorough gladness to set eyes on each other again. Or so it felt to her before self-doubt called her presumptuous for assuming he felt the same things.

"Okay, Sherlock, what's up?" she asked.

"I suspect the product is being taken out of the factory at night. I put a little listening device in the men's room and got a hint today that something might happen tonight."

Annie was impressed. "Wow. High tech. Just the men's room?"

"Call me chauvinist, but it seems more likely men

would be involved. Some of that furniture's pretty heavy."

"True."

"I thought we could park somewhere close and walk in," he said. "That way no one will realize we're there."

"I'm all yours."

It was one of those slips-of-phrase she instantly wished she could take back. That was until she glanced up to find his gaze on her, and felt, maybe for the first time in her life, the heady sense of power a woman feels when she knows a man wants her.

She smelled so damn good.

Jack knew her scent now. Some soft, subtle perfume—he had no idea what kind—but it made him think of spring flowers, sunshine and making love. And not necessarily in that order.

From here on out, he could be any place in the world, smell that perfume, and it would be Annie he thought of.

Annie, who was now sitting in the seat beside him, rigid as a flagpole, hands clasped in her lap.

At some point along the way, things had taken a turn between them. Headed toward something that had the feel of inevitability to it and filled him with the conflicting urge to run and to stay.

Stay had a stranglehold on him at the moment.

He could have gone to the factory alone tonight. Pretty much no getting around that fact. And even after all the arguments against doing so—each of which he'd held up for his own consideration—he'd reached for the phone and called her, the words just there as if someone else were saying them.

He turned the Porsche onto a narrow dirt road a quarter mile or so from C.M.

"Deep undercover?" Annie was smiling.

"Deep. I've got our camouflage gear in the back."

"What!"

"Kidding," he said.

"Good. Mud-green and brown are not my colors."

"Then that would have been a disaster," he teased.

A strip of woods lay between them and the factory. The building was just visible through the tall old oaks and maples.

"Are we walking through there?" Annie asked, sounding skeptical.

"Do you mind?"

She worried her bottom lip with small white teeth. "Ah, what about snakes?"

"It's September. Probably not too many out now."

"One is too many."

He looked down at her shoes, perfectly sensible running shoes beneath a pair of faded blue jeans. Which he took a moment to admire. He'd heard a lot of women say they didn't wear jeans because it took a teenager to look good in them. Not so for Annie. She looked good in them. She should live in blue jeans. "I've got on boots," he said, looking down at the old pair of Ropers. "No snake'll get through these."

"You think one could bite through mine?" She held up one foot at an angle, looking down at the shoes as if they'd already failed her.

"You really don't like snakes, do you?"

She shook her head. "It's my one concession to terror. When I was a little girl, I stuck my hand in a hen's nest at my grandparents' farm looking for eggs. There happened to be a snake in there doing the same thing."

"Did it bite you?"

"On the finger. I nearly died before they got me to the hospital."

A shaft of something not immediately identifiable hit him in the chest. A mingled combination of fear and relief. It took a few seconds for words to surface. "Okay," Jack said, clapping his hands together. "No walking through the woods for you tonight. Come on, I'll be carrying you."

"What?" The question came quickly enough that Jack knew it had caught her completely off guard. "No, that's all right. I—"

"Piggyback. You've already witnessed what a good pack pony I am."

"Jack, really, I couldn't—"

But he wasn't taking no for an answer. "It's not that far, and you'll be glad. You won't have to think about what's beneath every crunch of leaves."

She shivered, clearly torn. "Why don't I just wait here? I could be a lookout."

"But I need you over there. Come on," he said, turning around and bending his knees.

"Oh, goodness. Are you sure?"

"Positive."

There was probably only one thing in the world that would have made Annie climb on his back just then. And the thought of stepping on a snake was obviously it. With reluctant movements, she lifted one leg, clamped it to his waist, then gave a little jump onto the small of his back, hooking the other leg in place. "This is terrible," she said.

"What's so terrible?" He stood up, boosted her into place and started walking.

She gave a little shriek and then, "Maybe I should just walk."

"Your ticket's been punched. No getting off now." He could feel the stiffness of her posture. "Annie, you can relax, I won't break."

"I am relaxed."

He laughed. "If I run us into a tree limb, you're going to break."

"I'm fine," she insisted.

A few more strides and then, "Annie."

"What?"

"I think you're in danger of toppling. Don't you want to put your arms around my neck?"

"Ah, no. This is good," she said, wobbling even as she made the declaration.

"Annie."

"Yes?"

"Put your arms around my neck."

She did so, with great reluctance.

"I don't bite," he said.

So did silence mean she disagreed? He had a feeling she wished she'd risked the snakes.

He was beginning to have his own doubts about the wisdom of his gallantry. If a piggyback ride could have a theme song, this one would have been Prelude to Torture. What had he been thinking? Traipsing through the woods with Annie wrapped around his waist, and the last thing, the last thing, he wanted to do was pull out his I-Spy hat.

He wanted to put her down and let the front side of his body get to know her as well as his lucky back was getting to know her. The legs currently clinging to him were lean, but soft in that woman's way, and his mind set up its own scenario with her wrapped around him in another position altogether.

Too long, Corbin. You have been out of the real world for too long.

Just when sweat began to break out on his forehead—and it wasn't from overexertion—the edge of the woods came into sight. Twenty feet or so, and they were on the grass bordering the edge of the factory.

"Okay," Annie said, sounding breathless. "That's good. I can walk now."

Jack released her, and she slid to the ground. "Is your back all right?"

"Fine," he said, deciding it was a good thing she hadn't asked about the rest of him.

CHAPTER THIRTEEN

IF ANNIE HAD TO swing from tree limbs to get back to the car, there was absolutely no way she would be getting on Jack's back again. Amazing that something so silly and fun for Tommy and the boys Jack had been carting around the other night could be for her one of the most sensual experiences she'd ever known.

Or maybe that just said something about the droughtlike conditions of her own love life.

True enough, she had no love life, which certainly put it up for drought status. But in all honesty? It wouldn't have mattered.

Jack was the most physically appealing man she'd ever known. His shoulders strong and wide. His torso defined with muscle. And he'd carted her through those woods as if he hadn't even known she was on his back.

Except, of course, for the stranglehold she'd had around his neck. Once she'd agreed to hold on, she'd been afraid to let go. Her fear of what might be on the forest floor beneath them was real. While that fear might have legitimized her hold on him, it did not explain the way her skin suddenly felt a thousand times more sensitive, or the distinct wave of weakness flowing through muscle and bone.

No, it did not explain that.

Clarice, Annie. Think about Clarice. Your sister.

There was a perfectly good explanation for her feelings. Just the very normal response of a woman whose husband had left her for a younger, sportier model. More than likely, she would have the same reaction to any man paying her more than casual attention.

Oh yeah, then why have you not even looked at another man this past year?

Point made.

But that didn't mean she had to give it the benefit of analysis.

"I was thinking we could find a spot on the other side of the loading dock doors," Jack said, drawing her attention back to the reason they were here. "There are a couple of big trees up there. I don't think anyone would spot us if we stay in the shadows."

Her expression must have put voice to her worry.

"No woods. Just a couple big trees. And besides, did I forget to mention I exude a special snake repellent?"

She smiled. "You don't smell anything like mothballs."

"Glad to know it," he said.

She laughed.

At the edge of the parking lot, he reached for her

hand, tugboated her across the ink-dark asphalt and up a short hill to the twin oaks he'd declared snake-free.

"Think we'll be concealed enough?" he asked, turning to look at her without letting go of her hand.

Annie struggled to concentrate on the question. Her focus had centered on the feelings emanating out from the juncture of their entwined fingers. "The perfect spot," she said, throwing a glance back at the loading dock doors, then opening her fingers and releasing her hand from his.

He looked at her, a few things going unsaid between them but clearly understood, nonetheless. They weren't touching, stood a good two feet apart, and yet a connection remained, beckoned more.

Annie backed up and stepped on a fallen limb. The resounding crack jolted her forward where she righted herself a scant couple of inches from his chest. She had to look up, up, to see the half smile on his face. He knew the effect he had on her.

And it amused him. Amused him!

She stepped back again, this time with tentative enough steps that she managed to put a couple of yards between them without embarrassing herself.

"Might as well make ourselves comfortable," he said, leaning against the oak and sliding to the ground, patting the spot beside him.

It would have looked ridiculous, opting for the trunk of the tree five feet from the one he'd chosen. Smart maybe, but obvious. So she gave her indifference a pep talk and joined him on the ground. She crossed her legs and folded her arms across her chest like a turtle retreating into its shell, no vulnerable parts showing.

"So what do we do now?" she asked, aiming her tone at seriousness.

"Wait."

"And what do we do if they come?"

"Hadn't decided on that yet."

"You're not going to confront them tonight, are you?" Annie's eyes widened while a whole batch of less-than-comforting scenarios marched themselves out in 3-D, complete with gunshot sound effects.

"Depends on how many of them there are."

"Jack!" Her one-word protest echoed disbelief.

"Can't just let them get away."

"You're almost enjoying this, aren't you?"

"It's the cowboys and Indians thing," he said, his dark eyes crinkled at the edges.

"Except they'll probably arrive with a covered wagon full of shotguns, and we don't have a single tomahawk."

Jack laughed, and the sound of it sent a thrill of something deeply satisfying right through Annie's heart. It pleased her, making him laugh. Something so simple, and yet reaffirming, a check mark, audible proof of approval.

Sound played out in the night around them. Leaves crunching somewhere behind. A deer, maybe? A tractor from the dairy farm bordering the C.M. land.

Cows calling out to one another, their moos plaintive and questioning.

Annie focused on the loading dock parking lot in front of them, knowing, however, that Jack's gaze was on her. Her skin felt it, stung in the places it touched her. Like marbles on a hardwood floor, anticipation scattered through her, decimating any strands of logic she might have been clinging to. Did he want to kiss her? Was that the source of the almost tangible awareness hanging between them like thunder clouds full to bursting?

And she wished, deeply, for the answer to be yes.

"Annie?"

"What?" Her voice was so low she barely heard herself.

"I'd really like to kiss you."

Gladness grappled for footing, elbowed reason out of the way. "Are you asking permission?"

"I'm asking permission."

The request should have required, at the least, a little consideration on her part. Some mulling of consequence.

"Permission granted," she said, her voice again little more than a whisper.

Across the leaves he slid. Close enough, he angled his head, but made no further move to fulfill the request. Just studied her, long and hard. Annie had never been looked at in quite that way before. As if he were seeking to know her, really know her, take in some part of her she had never allowed anyone else to access. Under his appraisal, some part of her opened, wilted, weakened, and out leaked admission of her own need for this, yearning so real, so bone-deep she had no hope of hiding it.

"Annie." His voice sliding across her name confirmed it. He knew.

Her eyes closed, and he kissed her. A soft introduction of kisses that brought from her small sounds of wanting she wasn't aware she made. And then his arms circled her, pulled her straight against him, tight and hard, enclosed her in an embrace that said a dozen things about where it might go from there.

Annie melted into him, like chocolate put to heat, like snow under sun.

His hand went to her cheek, a brush of a touch, the pad of his thumb rough in the way of hands that are used, not pampered. The kiss, starting out with the reserve of introduction, changed tone, deepened, angled for something more intimate, found it in her willingness. Annie opened to him, realizing, only in doing so, that she'd lived the last year of her life curled around herself like an early spring flower bracing against one last reach of winter, and here it was at last, a true change in season, warmth, soft breezes, blue skies, a May afternoon.

And wasn't this what a kiss was supposed to be? Saying a thousand different things at once, that it had been thought about, hoped for, long before it ever became reality.

Everything about it felt like a first, first bicycle

solo—look, no hands!—first lick of a double scoop ice cream cone on a July day. First kiss. At its edges, relief that it was as good in reality as it had been in anticipation. And at the edges of Annie's heart, amazement, that she could incite such feelings in this man.

''Annie,'' he said again, and her name, plain as it was, on his lips sounded like that of a temptress, someone far more capable of seduction, of allure, than she had ever imagined herself to be. And at the look in his eyes, weighted as it was with impossible-to-deny wanting, she felt capable of those things, a woman in whom this man saw something no other man had ever seen in her, she had never seen in herself.

Her hands unbraced themselves from his chest, sought anchorage around his neck, and they changed leads, Annie kissing him now, making vulnerable a part of herself she had kept under lock and key for a long time, her husband's infidelity having diluted her own sense of appeal to the opposite sex.

Here, in this moment, she felt invulnerable, buoyed by the affirmation in his touch. What pleasure there was in the notion of being wanted, of feeling its existence in touch and embrace.

He let her lead, took for the moment the more passive role while she explored the appealing planes of his face, angle of jaw, breadth of shoulder. And when shyness, reserve, slowed her steps, he took the lead again, whirling her round a room of dizzying proportion, covering its vastness with perfectly attuned rhythm, timing. So in sync were they that it felt to Annie as if they'd been here before, danced this floor in some distant time, or had simply awaited its arrival for so long that its patterns were imprinted on heart's memory.

A truck growled up the road beside the factory, its descent in gears bringing them both back to the reason they were here. Lights flickered their way, and Annie craned for a glimpse of the gate at the factory's entrance.

"It's turning in," she said.

"Looks like it," Jack agreed.

There was disappointment in both their voices. The truck's appearance toppling the walls temporarily erected to the rest of the world. Reality was back, and with it, a wish for resolution of what they'd started, mingled with certainty that had it not appeared, they might have found exactly that.

Awkwardness, not unexpected, caught Annie in its grip. She was not a casual woman, and her life was not filled with scenes of this sort.

"Can I say something I probably shouldn't?" Jack asked.

Annie nodded. Words suddenly seemed to require effort beyond her capability.

"I've been wanting to do that since the first night we met when you walked into that diner looking ten kinds of flustered."

"It showed, huh?"

"A little," he said, and his smile was amused, but in the way of a man who thinks something is adorable, not ridiculous.

And then she refocused on the first part of what he'd said. He'd been thinking about kissing her since then? Annie's gaze dropped to her lap. What did she do with that? If she'd been conjuring up her own set of hopeful what-ifs, it would never have occurred to her to start with that.

"And one other thing," he said, reaching out to tip her chin up, forcing her to look at him.

"What?"

"It was worth the wait."

Annie wished for a quick wit, for flippancy. But felt neither amused nor flippant. Instead, she felt sobered and respectful of her own reaction to what they had just let happen between them. And joyful, yes, that most intensely, to know that this man to whom she could no longer deny her attraction wanted her. Wanted *her*.

Her own reply, should she have been able to find one, lost its opportunity when the truck turned in at the factory entrance. The gate was closed. Someone got out of the passenger door, a very tall man it appeared from here, and opened it. The truck pulled through, and he closed it again, then climbed back in.

"Let's get down," Jack said and stretched out on his belly.

Annie did the same, twigs snapping beneath her and what felt like an acorn pressing into her thigh.

They watched, silent now, while the truck made a U-turn and then backed up, the loud beep-beep of reverse ceasing when it eased to a stop against the thick black bumpers beneath one of the loading dock doors.

Both men got out. One pointed something at the door—a remote control, maybe?—and it opened.

"Do you know who they are?" Annie whispered.

"I can't get a clear look at their faces. They look familiar to you?"

"Not yet."

A minute or two ticked by. One of the men hoisted himself onto the dock entrance, disappeared inside, and then lights flared on. He appeared again, saying something to the man still standing beside the truck. From this distance, they couldn't hear what he was saying, but the light struck his face, and Annie gasped.

"Early Gunter," Jack whispered.

"But he's your security guard. Maybe they're here for something else."

"Maybe," he said. "But what?"

Good question. It was after ten o'clock on a week-night, and they'd just driven in here with an unmarked moving-van-type truck. It was hard not to draw conclusions. "I know Early well. And his family, too."

Jack sighed, that alone conveying his dismay. "You know, I was really hoping I was wrong on this."

"Me, too. In fact, I was sure you would be. But I

would never have believed Early capable of stealing.''

For the next forty-five minutes, they remained where they were, stretched out flat on the ground, watching while Early and the other man whom they had not been able to identify, carried product out of the warehouse and loaded it onto the truck. When they'd finished, they turned off the lights, closed the loading dock door, jumped back inside the cab and roared off.

''We've got to see where they're going with that,'' Jack said.

''You mean follow them?''

''Might not get another chance,'' he said.

As soon as they had closed the gate and started pulling away, he got to his feet and helped Annie up beside him. ''Come on,'' he said. ''You game?''

''Sure,'' she said and then remembered the return trip back through the woods and the snakes that were all surely in hibernation by now.

''Pony Express is still in service,'' he said, clearly reading her mind.

She held up a hand. ''No, no, really. A little desensitization will be good for me.''

''Sure you want to start your desensitizing tonight?''

''No time like the present.''

She wasn't fooling him. She could see it on his face, plain and clear. He knew exactly why she wasn't hoisting herself onto his back again. That was okay, though. There were some things imminently more dangerous to a girl's well-being than snakes.

THEY FOLLOWED THE TRUCK from a discreet distance for an hour and a half, down Route 220 South with its winding curves, across the Virginia border and into North Carolina.

Annie had made the trip through the woods like a hurdler in training, her feet so high off the ground her knees nearly hit chin level. Jack had led the way, and she was grateful for the simple fact that he hadn't looked back to see how ridiculous she looked.

Now, his expression grew more grim with every passing mile. Annie felt the direness of the situation, too; this was a man she knew, whose family she knew, chatted with in the post office, the grocery store. How could he drain the lifeblood from the company that had provided him a job for so many years?

"They're going to the first warehouse we went to, aren't they?"

"Looks that way." Jack's response sounded as if it had been dipped in concrete.

"Are you going to confront them?"

He shook his head. "No point in that. I'd like to get some pictures."

"What about calling the police?"

"I don't want to do that just yet."

"But they could catch them in the act of unloading."

"Yeah."

"You don't want to turn them in, do you?"

He ran a hand down his face, forehead to chin. "I don't hardly remember that place without Early being there. My father hired him because he had honest eyes. I'm having trouble believing he's in this alone."

"You think someone else at the factory is involved?"

"If I were betting, that'd be my guess."

"Any idea who?"

"Just hunches."

Annie didn't ask for names. She didn't really want to know them. It was disheartening to learn that people could be something so different from what they appeared to the rest of the world to be.

Just as they'd suspected, the truck took the exit they'd taken before, following the turns to the warehouse where they'd nearly gotten caught by the security guard.

Jack cut the lights, and they drove by the entrance, pulled over on a stretch of grass with a side view of the loading dock. Just as it had earlier, the truck backed up, the two men getting out and opening the warehouse door, then setting about the business of unloading.

Jack reached across the seat, popped open the glove compartment and pulled out a camera. His elbow brushed her knee on the trip back. Annie's reaction was instantaneous, that of someone who'd just walked into an unexpected stretch of electric fence.

"I'm sorry," he said.

"That's all right," Annie murmured, drawing up like a sand crab bent on escape. Only she had no place to go. Their eyes met for a moment, held, and something sparked between them, jolting through her with kick-start force.

Would he kiss her again? Did he want to?

She found herself hoping for yes as an answer to both, but he settled back in his seat, and the moment was gone, regret settling over her, seeping through skin and sinew.

He fiddled with the camera, checked for film. "Wait right here, okay? I'll be back."

"You're not going down there, are you?"

"No. Just close enough to get a few shots as evidence."

"What about the flash?"

"I'll take them fast. Can you get in the driver's seat and be ready to take off?"

"You have sleuthing in your blood, don't you?"

"Does that mean you think I'm good at it?"

"So far."

"Wish me luck," he said and ducked out of the car.

Annie got out and went around, sliding behind the wheel. She set the chronograph on her watch, then sat watching it tick off seconds, each one raising her adrenaline level to another peak. When they'd added up to twelve minutes, the tight little ball of panic in her stomach began to unravel.

She couldn't see him anywhere out there; the night

was tar-paper dark. What if they'd seen him? What would they do? Did they have guns?

Don't be ridiculous, Annie. Early Gunter may have turned out to be a thief, but he's not a murderer!

No sooner had doubt waged an assault on that particular assertion than the passenger door popped open and Jack jumped inside.

"Let's go!" he said.

Annie fumbled at the key, her fingers suddenly their own worst enemy. She turned it—finally!—shoved the gearshift into first and floored the accelerator.

They spun in the grass, then the tires caught the edge of the asphalt and shot them forward. Annie grappled with the wheel, the car veering right, then left like a sailor headed back to ship after a night in a port bar.

"Whoa," Jack said, "you're good at this. Where'd you learn to drive like that?"

"School of scared spitless."

Jack made a snorting noise and laughed a good belly laugh.

In spite of the fear that still had her in a choke hold, Annie smiled at the sound. "Did you get the pictures?"

"Enough I think," he said, exhaling another chuckle and settling back in his seat.

"Do you think they saw you?"

"Pretty sure they did."

Annie punched the accelerator, hurtling them down

the country road, aware of the injustice to the posted speed limit, but at the moment it seemed the lesser of two evils. "Are they following us?" She threw an anxious glance at the rear view mirror.

"Don't think so. They wouldn't stand a chance of catching us anyway."

She shot him a look. Saw the amusement on his face and let up on the accelerator. "Well, they could have been," she said.

"Yep." Another smile.

Warmth settled over Annie. A sense of something good and right. Of gladness for the company of a man who seemed to find things to appreciate about her. She could not remember the last time she had felt this way. Had she ever?

Silence stretched out between them for a mile or a few. It didn't matter because it was comfortable silence, companionable silence.

"Think they recognized you?" Annie asked after a while, tapping a thumb against the steering wheel.

"I doubt it. Might have gotten a look at the car."

"Hmm. So what're you going to do with the pictures?"

Jack sighed. "Wish I'd been wrong on this."

"What makes people justify embezzling?"

"Maybe they feel they've been shortchanged somehow. That they're owed something."

"But it's wrong."

"Yeah, it is."

"So what are you going to do?" she asked again, softly this time.

"I don't have a lot of choice," he said, regret in his voice.

"They haven't left you with any. That's for sure." The Porsche devoured a few more miles, and then Annie said, "Does this change anything for the future of C.M.?"

"I don't know, Annie," he said.

It wasn't much as hope went, but something inside her lightened with the words. Jack's answer held something it had never held before. Uncertainty.

CHAPTER FOURTEEN

IT WAS NEARLY MIDNIGHT when they pulled into Jack's driveway. Glad for the flexibility of her baby-sitter, Annie knew Mrs. Parker and Tommy both had long since gone to bed. The few times Annie had been out late for whatever reason, Mrs. Parker had slept in the guest bedroom, and since Annie didn't know what time she would be home tonight, they'd agreed Mrs. Parker would spend the night and go home in the morning.

Annie had driven the rest of the way home, the last part of the drive mostly silent, with a few bits of conversation sprinkled throughout.

Now that they were back, awkwardness settled around them, filling even the nooks and corners of the previous ease with which they'd laughed and talked and kissed, yes, kissed.

The night had served to make her forget about the situation with J.D., if only for a little while, and she had needed that.

"Thanks for going with me, Annie."

She reached for her purse, dug inside for her own car keys. "Could have done it on your own."

"It was nice to have the company."

The words had the ring of sincerity and something else, too. Unspoken though it was, clear reference to what had happened between them earlier. Annie heard it, felt it. Reveled a little in remembrance of it. Deliberately, during this last half of the night, she'd kept her thoughts away from those kisses, shooing them off with a determined mental broom, aware all the while, that later, in her own bed with the lights out, she would replay the scene. Relive it frame by frame. "I don't think it's exactly the right thing to say about a stakeout, but I had fun," she said.

"So did I."

They sat a while longer, let that settle, like cotton tossed to the wind, landing where it would. For Annie, it landed in her heart's corner, where seeds of happiness seemed intent on taking root in spite of the little voice that kept reminding her what a bad sister she was.

Who would have thought, a week ago when she'd been conjuring up all sorts of personalities for Jack Corbin, the man intent on draining dry a large part of Macon Point's livelihood, that she would end up here? With the very real desire to follow the path they'd started earlier tonight. See where it would end.

"Would you like to come in, Annie? Glass of wine?"

The questions hung there between them, enfolded in a thousand implications. A lethal blend of weakness and desire shot through Annie, finding little barrier in either muscle or resolve.

Just one. "Okay," she said.

He led the way to the front porch, unlocked the door and flipped on the foyer lights, wall sconces bathing the entrance in warmth. Jack led her into the kitchen, turned on another light and said, "Wait right here, I'll be back."

He disappeared through a door that went to the basement, judging from the sound of his footsteps on the stairs.

Annie stood by the window, looking out across the backyard. The horses were at the fence, staring at the house as if waiting for something. What was she doing here? Playing with fire. Hard to deny that.

The logical side of her brain said, "Go home, Annie. You have no idea what you're getting yourself into." The not-so-logical side said, "How often does a man like Jack ask you into his house for a glass of wine?"

Not very often, and she didn't see it changing in the future.

Annie did not think of herself as a sophisticated woman when it came to this kind of thing. She had married the only man she'd ever dated, never slept with anyone else. She was not by contemporary standards "experienced."

The realization did little, however, to still the feelings set astir inside her by the far too appealing way Jack kissed.

Heavens, could he kiss. Just the recollection of it made her mouth tingle, set into motion a cauldron of warmth that spread out from the center of her chest, intoxicating as any wine.

The basement door opened. She swung around, clearing her expression of memory.

He held up a bottle. "Port?"

"I've never had it."

"Try it?"

"Sure."

He went to an antique hutch in the corner of the kitchen, and pulled out two small wineglasses. He rummaged through a couple of drawers, found a cork-screw and opened the bottle, then poured them each a measure.

He handed her a glass and held his up, clinking the edge of hers. "To unexpected surprises, Annie. You have been an unexpected and very much appreciated surprise."

Annie tipped her glass up, a response completely eluding her. She turned to the window, grasped her glass between both hands, not knowing what to do with the words. "The horses. Do they always hang out at the fence when they see you come in?"

"I have to confess it's not me they like so much as the sugar cubes I've been giving them every night." His smile was chagrined, nearly boyish. An-nie's heart did another flip.

"Then we better take some out," she said.

Jack retrieved a yellow box from the pantry at the far corner of the kitchen. He held the back door open for her. They followed the brick walkway across the yard to the pasture. The horses whinnied at the sight of them. Stopping short of the fence, Jack set his wineglass on the ground, then shook loose some sugar cubes, holding out a hand for each horse.

They munched, both nodding their heads for more. Jack poured some out for Annie to give them, and she loved the feel of their soft muzzles against her palm.

She glanced up, found Jack's gaze on her, deep and penetrating as if he saw not what the rest of the world saw when they looked at her, but straight through to the heart of her, to her needs and wants, to what made her unique as a person. Special, even. As if he saw something in her no other man had ever taken the time to look for.

He leaned in then, slipped his arms around her waist and pulled her against him. It felt like the most natural thing in the world, as if, finally, she had found the man for whose embrace she had been custom-made. That was how well they fit, how right it felt to be against him, enfolded within lean, strong arms, secure, anchored.

And his kiss, ah, that. Annie had never before understood how a woman could lose her head, get so caught up in a man's embrace that she forgot to be careful, forgot to be cautious when one or the other was called for.

Now, she understood.

Caution was a filter through which all the arguments for sensibleness could be sifted. Sensibleness could be awfully boring.

Annie did not want to be sensible. Or boring. She'd been both for far too long.

Her wineglass slipped from her hand, fell to the ground.

Jack stepped back against the fence, brought her along with him in one deliberate motion. One boot on the bottom rail, he pulled her to him again, wedging her between his legs with an insistence that spoke of urgency and need, flattering both, this new angle taking to another level acknowledgement of their physical attraction.

Annie slipped her arms around his neck, opened her mouth to his, asking him to deepen the kiss. And he did, with a low sound of possession that sent a most feminine thrill of satisfaction straight out from the very core of her. She had never been kissed like this, wooed by a man's mouth to the point that all thought of anything remotely resembling resistance just fell apart into a million pieces, no longer identifiable.

There against the board fencing, they necked like teenagers, their skin heating up beneath the cool night air, his hands winding through her hair.

She could have stayed right here, just like this for the rest of her life and been quite happy about it.

"Annie, you feel so good."

"So do you," she said, the words the mildest of testimony to his effect on her.

Jack lifted the bottom of her sweater, his palm fitting to the curve of her waist. She felt his question, answered him with the slightest turn of her body; she wanted him to touch her, thought her heart might stop beating if he didn't.

He touched her breast, his hand closing round its fullness, thumb circling the tip through the lace of her bra. Like warm caramel, Annie went soft and liquid, drawn to him as if he had all the answers to every question she had not thought to ask.

Now, she not only wanted to ask them, but know the answers to each one as well.

"Annie?" Jack pulled back, brushed the back of his hand across her cheek, tipped her chin up with one finger.

"Hmm?"

"I'd really like to take you upstairs and make love to you."

"Jack?"

"Hmm?"

"I'd really like for you to take me upstairs and make love to me." Was that her voice, soft and husky? Had she really said that?

He waited a few seconds, as if giving her time to take it back. A dozen reasons for doing so scattered through her conscience. This is the man your sister wanted. *You're a mother, Annie.* What are you thinking?

But she was a woman, too. With wants and needs of her own. And for whatever reason, fate had steered them all toward this man, this moment. And she simply wanted.

So she didn't take it back.

Jack dipped down, scooped her up. Annie slipped her arms around his neck. She was a tall woman. She'd always envied petite women for the fact that they never had to worry during moments like this whether the man might regret his gallantry.

But judging from the precision of Jack's stride, she might have weighed no more than a bag of feathers. She felt feminine in a way that has nothing to do with a woman's shape or size, but with the fact that she is the focus of one man's desire.

Across the yard they went. Through the back door. Then the kitchen. And up the wide staircase.

She should say something. Because, really, shouldn't this feel awkward or terrifying at the least?

It didn't. It felt right, as if this night could not have ended in any other way.

At the top of the stairs was a very long hallway. He turned into the second room on the right and kicked the door shut behind him.

Only then did he put her down, not, she quickly discovered, from sudden onset exhaustion, but an apparent immediate need to kiss her again. Annie kissed him back. Kissed him with honest, openhearted emotion. Vulnerable though it made her, it was what she felt. A more sophisticated woman might have tempered it with coyness or something at least resembling mystery.

But that wasn't Annie. And she'd never been very good at trying to be something she wasn't. Still, old doubts weren't easily dispelled. "Jack?"

"Jack here."

"I…" Awkwardness locked the words in her throat. "I've never thought of myself as very gifted in this department. I mean J.D. and I never had much fun together that way."

"Does that mean the sex wasn't great?"

Annie started to sidestep the question, then opted for honesty again. "Actually, that would be a generous assessment."

"Annie," he said, his palm curving around her neck, his smile appreciative in a way she couldn't quite pinpoint, knew only that it softened the edges of her apprehension. "Then you weren't with the right man."

She was going to wake up at any moment. It would be the middle of the night, and the TV would be blaring. And this would all be just a very nice dream.

But then he kissed her again, and all thoughts of why or why not, of anything other than the here and now drifted out of reach. And there was only this. This man who kissed like he'd been made for that sole purpose, brought feeling whirling up from every extremity and centered it at her heart's core.

For a long time, they stood by the moon-draped bed, kissing, finding their way. He lifted her sweater, pulled it over her head, dropped it on the chair beside them. "You're beautiful," he said.

The words sent another wave of warmth coursing through her, and for the first time in her life, she felt beautiful. She put her hands on his chest, began unbuttoning his shirt, the backs of her fingers grazing the skin beneath, each touch tightening the knot of desire between them until she could no longer draw full breath. She felt as if her very bones had weakened, might no longer hold her up.

But Jack swooped her up again, placing her, this time, on the poster bed in the center of the room. Annie sank into the thick down comforter, unable to take her gaze off him.

"Are you sure, Annie?"

Annie didn't want to think about tomorrow or yesterday. What might have been or what might be. Just this. And what they had found in this night. "I'm sure," she said.

THEY LAY ENTWINED, Annie's head on his chest, one leg curved around his.

The moon had lifted its beam, aimed it at the corner of the room, draping the bed in shadow.

"Annie?" Jack's voice was husky around the edges.

"Annie here."

"You're gifted."

She tucked her face against his chest, smiled against his bare skin. And one thing she now knew to be true. Jack was right. She had not been with the right man.

LATER, MUCH LATER, they made use of the closet-size shower in Jack's bedroom, turning an ordinary daily ritual into something so pleasurable, it was nearly impossible for Annie to get dressed and leave. Likewise the kiss he left her with after walking her out to the car and tucking her inside.

He pulled back and held her gaze for a long moment, his hand lingering on the side of her face. "This wasn't casual for me, Annie."

She pressed her lips together, the words tying a knot around her heart. "Me, either."

"So what happens now?"

"One day at a time?"

He considered that, nodded once. He closed the door and stepped back.

And Annie drove home, hopeful that this was as real as it felt.

A STRANGE CAR SAT in the driveway of her house. Annie pulled the Tahoe in behind it, frowning. Where was Mrs. Parker's car? This one had the generic look of a rental. Alarm threaded through her, hastening her steps up the brick walkway. She dropped her keys just as she reached the front door.

She bent down, picked them up, and straightened to find the door open and J.D. standing on the other side. Looking as polished and magazine-perfect as J.D. always looked. The L.A. sun had lightened his hair a couple of degrees, and his face was tan against his white shirt.

She dropped the keys again.

He bent to pick them up this time and handed them to her.

She took them from him with a hand responding on automatic pilot. "What are you doing here?" she asked, icicles inserting themselves in the question, even as she fought for neutrality.

"Visiting," he said. "Come in."

"Where is Mrs. Parker?"

"I sent her home."

"You what?" Stunned, she stood there, feet bolted to the porch floor.

"Didn't see any need in her staying when I was here."

Outrage sent a flare to her feet, propelling her through the front door and into the living room where she turned and glared at him, hands balled into fists at her hips to prevent them from shaking. "How dare you come in this house and start issuing orders you have no right to issue?"

He leaned a shoulder against the doorjamb, hands shoved in the pockets of his jeans, his feet bare. "It was my house, too."

"Was, J.D. Was."

"But Tommy is still my son, and I ought to have the right to spend time with him alone when I haven't seen him in months."

Annie could practically feel steam emanating from her skin. "And whose fault is that?"

He shrugged a J.D.-identifying shrug, a lift of one

shoulder, a tilt of his head, and the message was the same as always: not his.

Annie tossed her purse on the couch, folded her arms across her chest. "I'd like for you to leave, J.D."

"Be reasonable, Annie. It's the middle of the night. Where would I go this late?"

"You can sleep in your car for all I care! You are not invited to spend the night in this house."

He smiled. Smiled! As if he found this whole thing greatly amusing. Annie felt close to boiling.

"You look different, babe."

"I let my hair grow, J.D. Now that we've established that change, please leave."

He crossed the room, not stopping until he stood bare toes to the tip of her shoes. He reached out and wound a strand of her hair around his finger. "I like it. A lot."

There had been a time when that look on his face, that suggestion in his voice would have toppled Annie's anger with him. She waited now, some part of her curious. Would it still be there? Did she still need his approval, assurance that he found her attractive?

She stepped back.

He followed.

"I've missed you, Annie."

"And what exactly brought that on, J.D.? Looking for a way to make your teeny-bopper girlfriend go away?"

"You didn't used to be sarcastic."

"No, but I used to be a lot of other things. Naive, for one."

"So I've made you jaded, is that it?"

"That would mean you have power over me, J.D. And you do not. You do not."

"Really?" He stepped forward again, following her until she reached the wall behind her. His arms made brackets on either side of her. He leaned in until his face was inches from hers. "Like to prove it?"

He was going to kiss her. She bridled at the idea. But something inside her said, okay, prove it. Are you really and truly over him? Show him. Show yourself.

He leaned in, tested her mouth with a quick kiss. She didn't respond. He looked down at her with a raised eyebrow. Then leaned in again, his mouth taking hers in a kiss of another kind, just as he had obviously taken her silence as acquiescence.

When, in actuality, it had been consideration. Appraisal of her own reaction. Or the absence of one.

And suddenly, she recognized his kiss for what it was. What it had always been. Practiced. Perfected. Mechanical to her now. J.D.'s kisses had always had a purpose. Don't be mad at me, Annie. I won't do it again.

Her thoughts turned to another kiss. Another man whose touch had felt like something else altogether. Not practiced. Not even perfect. Too imbued with what had felt like genuine need to care whether their noses bumped.

The only genuine need in J.D.'s kisses was that

behind whatever his current agenda was. And he always had one. Always.

Annie pulled back, turned her head away. ''J.D., stop.''

''Annie, sweet Annie, I've missed you. And Tommy.'' His lips found her neck, gave it a teasing nip.

''Stop,'' she said and pushed him away.

It was not the response he'd been hoping for. His expression said so clearly. This was his hurt-little-boy face, the one he'd always pulled out whenever he thought he had a pretty good chance of changing her mind.

She had news for him: this time it wasn't going to work.

''Please, leave, J.D. You can come back in the morning, and we'll talk.''

''Okay, I can understand you're not going to forgive me so easily. I'm willing to work at it.''

''There's nothing to work at. What do I have to say to make you understand that?''

He dropped into the leather chair by the fireplace. ''If that's how you want it, Annie, then here's the deal. I want my son back. In my life every day. The choices are pretty clear. Either we get back together, and we both have him, or we don't, and I'll find a way to make a court see that he should be with me.''

ANNIE GAVE IN AND let J.D. stay in the guest room. The night was half over anyway, and she was too shell-shocked by the ultimatum he'd just given her to put up much of an argument.

After checking on Tommy, she'd gone to her room—locking the door—washed her face and put on pajamas. She climbed in bed and sat with her back to the headboard, her heart throwing itself against the wall of her chest.

J.D. had lost his mind. That had to be it. There was no other explanation for what had just happened.

She waited to feel something, anything, but there was just this awful numbness inside her, leeching outward until even her fingers and toes felt brittle with it. Her thoughts chased one another in circles, leading nowhere.

What would she have said had he come back a year ago, six months ago? Would she have forgiven him? Wanted him back?

Be honest, Annie. Would you?

Probably. There, that was honest.

She couldn't say for sure what her true motivation would have been—some leftover morsel of love for him, a desire to put their family back together again, or maybe pride and simply that, unadmirable though it was.

But now, she felt none of those things. They just weren't there anymore, like words on a blackboard, erased, gone.

And Jack. There was Jack. Jack, who made her laugh. Who asked her opinion as if the weighing of it were crucial in whatever decision he happened to be making. Who looked at her with eyes that reflected someone she had never imagined herself being to a man like Jack.

She had to believe he had come into her life for a reason. It was her nature to look at life's plot that way, put logic to what might otherwise be seen as coincidental, circumstantial, paths that appeared to veer off into confusing tangles having direction and destination all along. That did not mean she was presumptuous enough, confident enough, to assume there would be anything lasting in their temporary collision, of course.

But from it, she had already had her eyes opened to a few life-altering things. Yes, maybe a year ago she would have weakened to J.D.'s demand that they put their marriage back together. Come to the eventual conclusion that it would be best for Tommy, that maybe J.D. really would have changed this time. But not now. Now, she was someone different from the woman he'd married, a young, starstruck, I'll-make-him-happy wife who'd beaten her head against the wall of a doomed-from-the-start marriage until she'd come to see the resulting bruises as just part of her normal complexion.

A person didn't have to live that way. Shouldn't live that way. She hadn't been a perfect wife. There was no such thing, she was sure, and she certainly would never have nominated herself for the title. But she had tried. Tried a thousand different ways to make J.D. see her as enough. Enough of a wife that maybe

respect alone would keep him from straying. Enough
of a lover that his eyes did not inevitably stray to the
prettiest woman in the room at parties. But they did.
Always. And she knew now, if she had never ac-
cepted it before, that they always would.

Something else, she knew now, too, though. This
wasn't her fault. She was woman enough, pretty
enough, for someone. Not J.D., maybe. But the reason
for that she no longer laid at her own doorstep. J.D.'s
roving libido was the result of a flaw in him. Not her.
And for years, she had believed the opposite to be
true.

So maybe that was the reason Jack had been put in
her path. To show her a reflection of herself she had
not allowed herself to see before. She liked who she
was with him. A woman who laughed and made
laughter. A woman who flirted and was flirted with.

So what did all of this mean?

It meant that J.D. no longer had power over her.
The only reason he ever had was that she had given
it to him. Had allowed him to treat her as someone
unworthy of respect and fidelity. The thought was
freeing in that it was completely within her control to
never allow it to happen again. Why was it that something so seemingly simple had remained elusive to
her for the duration of her marriage?

The reason was simple. Because she had not
wanted to see it. Had wanted, instead, to believe herself unworthy of those things.

She was a different woman now. Had proved to

herself that she did not need J.D. to exist. That she was perfectly capable of making a life for Tommy and her that was full and fulfilling.

This time she would not bend. She was not giving up her son. Would fight him like a tigress whose cub was being threatened. And she was not going to allow J.D. to bully his way back into her life.

He had waged this particular battle with the advantage of surprise. Much as he had the end of their marriage. And while it was tempting to march down the hall, order him out of the house and out of her life, this was not a war she intended to lose, and for that she would need strategy. Strategy did not allow for the luxury of indignation.

The first thing she had to do was set things right with her sister. Now, like so many other times in her life, she was going to need her.

CHAPTER FIFTEEN

JACK COULD NOT SLEEP. Sleep had never been a problem for him. He could close his eyes in any airport,
on any train, and be out in two minutes.

But not tonight.

Tonight, he couldn't get his mind off Annie. Or the
memory of her upstairs in his bed.

Restlessness paced through him, its footsteps too
loud to ignore. So he got up and tried outpacing it,
roaming room to room in the big old house. But it
followed, and he finally ended up in his father's
study, with its now subtle clues of Joshua Corbin's
once-daily presence: the pipe he'd smoked in the evenings with its cherry-flavored tobacco, the shelves of
books on one wall, the spines still bookstore new, but
the pages within dog-eared and well-read.

Jack reached up, pulled a book from the shelf,
glanced at the title on the cover. It wasn't something
he'd ever heard of, but his father's taste in books had
run toward the adventuresome, tales of pioneer treks
across unforgiving mountain ranges and the hurdles
to be cleared before making a home on the other side.

He sat down in the leather chair by the window,
flicked on the floor lamp beside it. He opened the

book, met in the first paragraph the story's young heroine, but his thoughts strayed, unfaithful, to another woman.

Annie.

He let the book drop forward and find a resting spot against his chest. He closed his eyes and replayed the night. Saw the two of them traipsing through the woods, Annie on his back, legs and arms wrapped around him as if he were the last safe haven in the path of a killer storm.

The appeal of that hit him like the sharp crack of a whip.

Annie struck chords never before played inside him. Made him feel things he'd never felt before.

Making love to her had been like rediscovering the experience for the first time. With Annie, everything felt like the first time. With all the excitement and uncertainty that go with it.

Sitting there in his father's study, Jack knew he had found the woman with whom he wanted to spend his life. Knew it in the farthest reaches of heart and soul, in that place where the deepest truths make themselves known.

Annie was the woman he'd never imagined meeting. Never imagined wanting in a way that told him his life was never going to be the same without her in it.

He could list a dozen reasons why it would never work. They didn't live in the same place…he was supposed to start a new project in London as soon as he tied things up here…she'd been hurt by a man who had not appreciated her for the woman she was….

But Jack closed his mind to them all. Somehow, he knew there was no roadblock he couldn't figure out how to get them around. He'd just take them on one by one and see where they led.

CLARICE CRACKED AN EYE at her alarm clock. Nearly nine. Darn, she'd overslept. No wonder, though, since it had been nearly four before she'd managed to fall asleep. She got up, flopped downstairs to make coffee in a posture her mother would have once called sulky. Clarice considered herself a big enough woman to admit her mother would have been right. For two days now, that was exactly what she'd been doing: sulking.

She scooped some beans out of the container in the freezer, put them in the coffee grinder. She'd spent all of last night simmering in front of the TV. Stoking her indignation like a campfire she refused to let go out, using, as kindling, her own well-justified arguments as to having voiced right up front her intentions where Jack Corbin was concerned.

The downside about being mad at her sister was that she was the one person Clarice would have liked to call up and complain to about it.

The doorbell rang. She swung back through the kitchen to answer it, not caring that she hadn't yet brushed her hair or removed the mascara from beneath her eyes. On the front porch stood Annie, arms folded across her chest in a stance that said okay-let's-have-it-out.

"Annie," Clarice said, eyes widening.

"Okay, let's have it out," Annie said and marched past her into the kitchen.

Whoa. Clarice trailed after her.

Annie went straight to the coffeepot, poured herself a cup and sipped at it, her eyes lasering in on Clarice over the rim. "You've been avoiding me," she said. "Not taking my calls. Don't you think it's time we dealt with this?"

Clarice's jaw went slack. Annie had never spoken to her this way. She was the one who ought to be in the driver's seat. She was the one whose pride had been injured. With an indifference she didn't quite feel at the moment, Clarice eased across the kitchen floor and poured herself a cup of coffee. "I never imagined you as capable of being underhanded."

"Underhanded?"

"I think leading me to believe you weren't interested in Jack when you really were seems a little underhanded."

"Clarice, I wasn't."

"Aren't?"

Annie looked down. "I didn't mean to be."

Clarice's heart did a little dip. "So why couldn't you just admit you wanted him?"

"Clarice." Annie deflated, as if someone had stuck a pin in the dukes-in-the-air determination she'd sailed in on. The look on her face told Clarice everything she needed to know. No matter what Annie said from this point forward, Clarice knew her sister. She was in love with Jack. No question about it.

"So this is my payback for Craig Overby, huh?"

Annie glanced up, visibly surprised by the name. "You've never mentioned him once in all these years."

"Maybe I was too ashamed. I was a bad sister. You had already staked that claim."

"And you think I've been a bad sister now?"

Clearly, there were two roads Clarice could take from here. High or low. There were times when she had taken advantage of her sister's dislike of conflict between them. Used it to come out the winner of whatever it was they were at odds over. She could have done it this time as well. Annie was that loyal. Selfishness died an unwilling death inside her, sending out a last flare of reason: You wanted him, though!

True, she had.

But the truth had not changed. He wasn't interested in her. He was interested in Annie. Painful as it was to admit. She sighed and said, "Oh, Annie, I've been a total boar's behind."

Relief danced across Annie's face like sunshine. "Well, maybe not quite that bad."

"Close enough for comparison. So this makes us even on the whole Craig thing, right?"

Now Annie laughed. She crossed the kitchen floor,

put her arms around Clarice and hugged her. "You know I think you walk on water."

The words filled Clarice with warmth and gratitude. She was lucky to have a baby sister who simply loved her for who she was. She'd been foolish to take it for granted. "I'm sorry, Annie."

"I'm sorry, Clar."

They hugged each other for a long grateful moment, and when they pulled back, Clarice swiped at a tear on her cheek. "I guess I've just started to feel a little desperate. Like I'm never going to meet anyone I could spend the rest of my life with. Have children with."

"You will," Annie said softly. "Don't ask me how, but I just know it."

And hearing her little sister say the words with such absolute conviction, Clarice believed them herself.

CLARICE WENT UPSTAIRS to get dressed. Annie put away the last of the dishes in her sister's sink, grateful that the two of them had straightened things out. Clarice was such an important part of her life. Without her, everything felt out of balance, off-center. Annie still felt the fissure that separated what had once been solid ground between them, but she was hopeful that if they both followed the edges of it, somewhere ahead it would merge back into one path again. Regardless of what happened between Jack and her.

Clarice reappeared in the kitchen doorway, now

dressed in jeans and a light green blouse. "So are you going to tell me what else is bothering you?"

"J.D. wants Tommy," Annie said.

Clarice blinked, her lips making an O of surprise. "He's worse than San Francisco fault lines. Always trying to shake things up."

"He's serious this time, Clar. He was at my house last night when I got home. With an ultimatum. Either we get back together, or he'll find a way to get sole custody of Tommy."

Clarice looked as shocked as Annie had felt last night. "What happened to L.A. and his barely legal Cassie?"

Annie shrugged. "You know J.D. He has the attention span of a gnat."

"So what's behind all this?"

"I don't know," Annie said, her voice failing to hide the distress her heart felt. "He says he misses Tommy. And me."

"I don't doubt that for a minute, but with J.D., isn't there always an agenda other than the immediately obvious?"

"He thinks he's had some sort of epiphany. Realized what he's thrown away. He wants another chance at being a good father, a good husband. Thinks he never really gave either his best effort because he was distracted with his career and then with his injury. He says he's ready now to be a pro at both."

Clarice chewed her bottom lip; her eyes widened

with what looked like a moment of inspiration. "So then let him."

Annie frowned; it was not the response she had expected from the sister who had practically stood at the county line waving good riddance to J.D. when he'd left Macon's Point. "Clarice, there is no way I'm letting him back into my life."

"Not permanently. Just temporarily. Just long enough to drown him in domesticity and all the things he's convinced himself he now wants. To let him hang himself, as they say. He claims to want all of those things, so let him prove it."

Annie pondered the suggestion, struck with the inspiration of it. J.D. was one of those people for whom revelations had to come from within. Unless it was his idea, his emotion, he didn't trust it. "What if it doesn't work, though?"

"Then you'll have to fight it out in court. Which is where you're headed right now, anyway."

The thought of that made Annie's stomach turn. She'd gotten a very large dose of just how ruthless that process could be during their divorce. She did not want to test the waters of the legal maneuverings involved in a custody battle. Dragging Tommy through that would be her worst nightmare.

So what did she have to lose in trying this route first?

JACK DROVE THROUGH town that morning with his thoughts all tied up in the meeting ahead. A couple

of discreet phone calls had revealed that today was
Early Gunter's day off. Which made sense considering the late hour he'd undoubtedly arrived home last
night.

One hand on the wheel, he took another jump
through the set of possible actions he could take from
here. None of them was remotely palatable. And all
led back to the same beginning. He had no choice but
to do something.

The easiest response would have been involving
the police. To do so would have meant keeping his
own hands clean as far as confrontation went. But one
thing had changed since he'd come back to Macon's
Point: he cared what happened to that factory. He'd
awoken to that realization this morning, its existence
clearly etched in his conscience. He cared. Didn't
want to see it sucked down the pipes of bankruptcy
like so much dishwater.

Corbin Manufacturing had made a difference in the
lives of a lot of people. Still could. That was the part
he could no longer ignore. Annic's efforts at person-
alizing the situation had worked. When he thought of
the company now, he saw individual faces, recognized what the demise of the business would mean to
each of them, to this town.

And so he'd called Early, asked him to meet him
in the parking lot of the old Second Baptist Church
off Elm Hollow Road. A startled Early had agreed on
the phone. Question was, would he follow through?

Nothing about this meeting held the mark of anything Jack would normally have done. He should have decided ahead what he was going to say. Let someone know where he was in case anything went wrong. But he hadn't done any of that. He wanted to hear what Early had to say for himself. Eye to eye. Man to man.

They'd agreed to meet in the church's back parking lot. Jack was ten minutes ahead of schedule. He drove around the side of the building. Early was already there. Pacing the width of an old blue pickup and puffing on a cigarette hard enough to suck the whole thing down his throat.

Jack parked beside him, got out, kept his expression neutral. "Hey, Early."

"Jack." The nod was curt, but the look in his eyes was pure terror.

"Guess you know why I called."

Early shrugged. "That you out there last night?"

Jack nodded.

Early dropped the cigarette, ground it out with the scuffed toe of his work boot. "So what're you plannin' to do about it?"

"Thought I'd ask you the same."

"Ain't much I can do."

Jack leaned back against the hood of Early's old truck, hung a heel on the front bumper, folded his arms across his chest. "Guess I don't see it that way."

"What is it you do see?"

"I'd like to think a mistake."

Early hung his head. "Don't matter what you call it if it's wrong, and you can't go back and redo it."

"How'd you get in this mess, Early?"

"Weakness, I guess."

Jack respected that answer. A lot of men would have thrown out a list of excuses that had nothing to do with their own responsibility. "Would you redo it if you could?"

Early looked up, met Jack's direct gaze, his eyes wavering, then snapping back and holding their ground. "Reckon I would."

"My father thought you were a good man. Not once in my life did I ever know him to be wrong on that. Was he wrong this time?"

Early's face, weathered, time-worn, held the clear footprints of shame. And regret.

"One thing was true about my father, Early. He knew how to judge a man's character. I don't think he was wrong about you. And that's what tells me you would never have started this thing on your own. You want a chance to make this right, you're gonna have to tell me who did."

THEY'D TALKED FOR over an hour. Gone over from the beginning when the stealing had started, how long it had been going on. And Early had given him names. The two that counted. One was Hugh Kroner. This did not surprise Jack.

Hugh and the other man were educated, highly paid executives who had embezzled from the company with deliberate intent. Jack could not excuse Early's role in the situation. But if he called in the police on the other two, Early would go to jail as well. Maybe that would have been the right thing. Maybe Jack was being too soft.

He hadn't promised Early anything. Had just told him he had a lot of thinking to do and that he would be in touch. Early had given him his word he would not betray him by letting the others involved know of their meeting.

Now, headed back toward town, there was one person, and only one, with whom he wanted to share all this. And that was Annie.

J.D. PACED THE WIDTH of Annie's living-room floor like a cat someone had forgotten to let out for its daily prowl.

He glanced at his watch. Where was that boy? "Tommy," he called up the stairs. "Hurry up now, or I might have to find somebody else to throw ball with today."

"Coming, Dad," he yelled back, panic in his voice, his footsteps thumping faster on the wood floor of his bedroom.

A car pulled up outside and shut off its engine.

J.D. went back to the window. Annie, probably. Maybe he could talk her into a little bedroom reunion before he and Tommy headed for the park.

But the vehicle outside was a black Porsche. A man got out. Well, well.

J.D. slicked a hand across his hair, shot a glance in the foyer mirror, then went to open the door.

Jack Corbin looked surprised to say the least. He caught it fast though, and said, "Annie home?"

"Not right at the moment," J.D. said, assessing the other man without moving his gaze below his face.

"Been a few years," Corbin said, sticking out his hand.

J.D. reluctantly stuck out his own. "Yeah. Annie went over to Clarice's. Should be back in a little while. Hear she's been trying to talk you out of closing your factory."

"We've been working on a couple things together."

"Well, no doubt, in this instance, she's been a more effective mayor than I would have been."

Corbin let that stand a moment and then, "In many, I'm sure."

"Since you and Annie have become friends, maybe you'd like to hear the good news. We're going to try and work things out. Figured out Annie's too good a woman to let go. And she's decided not to put Tommy in the middle of a messy custody battle."

If J.D. hadn't been looking for it, he might have missed the flare of emotion in Corbin's eyes. Small as the victory was, he enjoyed it. J.D. loved all wins, big and small.

Tommy thumped down the stairs. He stopped in the doorway beside J.D. and said, "Hi, Jack!"

"Hey, Tommy. Gonna play some ball with your dad today?"

Tommy nodded. "Wanna go with us?"

"Can't today, but thanks. Next time?"

Tommy nodded. J.D. put a hand on the boy's shoulder and pulled him in closer. "He's his father's boy."

Corbin held his gaze for a long moment, then said, "Have fun, Tommy." He got back in the Porsche and drove off.

J.D. looked down at Tommy. "He been around much?"

"He and Mama have been talking about bizness. He gave me a Hank Aaron card."

"That right?"

"Wanna see it?" Tommy pulled back and looked up at him, eagerness in his face.

"Nah. What do you need with a stupid old card when you've got the real thing?"

CHAPTER SIXTEEN

AFTER SHE LEFT Clarice's, Annie went to the office for a few hours, surely the most unproductive she'd ever spent there. The Lord's Acre Sale was set to take place tomorrow in the high school parking lot. In addition to sitting in the dunking booth, Annie had been asked to give a speech. She'd started seven different versions, each now residing in a wadded-up ball at the bottom of her trash can.

For the life of her, she couldn't concentrate.

Her emotions were like a seesaw with a bad spring, sending her zooming high and then plopping her down on the other side hard enough to loosen teeth.

The seesaw was Jack.

This was no time to be thinking about Jack.

So, of course, she could not stop thinking about Jack.

Her ex-husband had shown up on her doorstep out of the blue, intent on sending another wrecking ball through the center of her life. And every time she thought about Jack—just his name—she felt positively giddy inside, like a fourteen-year-old who's just kissed without braces for the first time and figured out that it's pretty darn incredible.

Kissing J.D., she realized now, had been like kissing with braces on.

Somehow, she had to make him see that he did not want his old life back.

A COUPLE OF HOURS LATER, she was in the kitchen making a pot of soup, beef barley which she happened to remember J.D. hated—salt made him bloat, and barley, what was that anyway, some kind of earth mother food?—when he and Tommy returned from the park.

The front door opened, and through it rolled the sound of Tommy's happy laughter. "Can you believe how far that ball went, Daddy?"

"You are gonna be something one day, son. No doubt about it," J.D. said.

Annie bit back the urge to run out and tell Tommy he already was something wonderful, that they didn't need to wait around for that to happen. *Stick to the plan, Annie.* She gave the pot of soup another shower of salt and threw in an extra handful of barley.

Cyrus got up from his spot at Annie's feet and galloped to the front door.

"Off, Cyrus," J.D. said. "Down, boy."

Annie pictured J.D. flattened to the foyer wall, Cyrus's paws planted on his chest in greeting. Good boy, Cyrus.

The three of them straggled into the kitchen then, Tommy's cheeks reddened by an afternoon outdoors, the look on his face one of such happiness that Annie teetered under the realization of how much he loved his father. Somehow, she had to keep her own agenda with J.D. separate from that. Tommy's need for his father's attention was something she was never going to be able to fill.

"Hey, you two," she said.

"Mama, you'll never believe what all we did today!"

"So tell me," Annie said.

"We went to the Dairy Queen, and I got two orders of fries and an extra large Coke!"

Annie smiled and raised her eyebrows, threw a look at J.D. who shrugged, innocent as ever. He looked a little rumpled around the edges. His short blond hair needed an appointment with a comb, and his white Hugo Boss T-shirt had a ketchup stain on the pocket.

Fatherhood did not come naturally to J.D.

Another image came to mind: Jack out in the backyard acting as pack pony for Tommy and his gang of friends. *Don't, Annie.* Not a good place to go right now.

Annie put a hand on Tommy's shoulder. "Tommy, why don't you go upstairs and change clothes before dinner?"

"'Kay," Tommy said and sailed off.

J.D. came into the kitchen, leaned over and kissed her cheek. "Um, whatcha got cooking?"

"Beef and barley," she said, picking up the spoon and giving it a stir.

Long pause. "Sounds great," he said.

Wow. He really was trying. "It'll be ready in a few minutes."

"So have you thought about our talk last night, Annie?"

"A little."

"And?"

"I think we should give it a try."

J.D. smiled a cat-who-ate-the-canary smile. He'd expected no less. Just the thought nearly made Annie toss the whole ridiculous farce just so she could tell him hell would freeze over twice before he ever crossed the threshold of her bedroom door.

"That's my girl," he said, reaching out to twine a finger through her hair.

Annie stepped back, made a pretense of reaching in the back of a drawer for a spoon. "Don't think this can just happen overnight, J.D."

"I know we have a lot of water under our bridge, Annie. But you've always been the kind of woman who could forgive and forget."

Doormat Annie again. The assessment made her steam inside and filled her with an urge to dunk his head in the pot of soup simmering on the stove.

"You had a visitor today," he said.

Annie swung around, something in the tone of his voice setting off alarm bells. "Who?"

"Jack Corbin."

Her heart did a three-sixty. She turned back to the stove. "Oh. What did he say?"

"Not too much. He didn't look all that thrilled to see me here."

Annie dipped out a spoonful of soup and sampled it, scorching her tongue which she didn't trust with words, anyway.

"I told him we were going to try and patch things up," J.D. said.

Annie whirled around, soup flying from the spoon to splatter his ketchup-tarnished T-shirt. "You what?"

He glanced down as he flicked the spots off. And after a few moments, "Well, there's no reason it should be a secret, is there?"

Annie put a clamp on her response while rebellion bucked inside her. Of all the absolute nerve! With his track record during their marriage, it surpassed all standards of arrogance for J.D. to go anywhere near the subject of her personal life when they were divorced. Divorced!

She popped open the cupboard door beside the stove and pulled out a bowl, filling it with soup. "Sit down, J.D.," she said in a sugar-infused voice. "Dinner's ready."

JACK DROVE OUT to the factory feeling as if he'd walked into a stone wall.

Annie was getting back together with J.D.

How could that be?

After last night—

And yet he'd seen the man standing in her house with his own eyes. Heard him say the words with his own ears.

When he was with Annie, for the first time in his life, he'd been blindsided by proof that maybe he'd been wrong all these years. He had never felt for anyone what he felt when he looked at Annie. As if he'd been given new eyes to see the world with, as if he could do things that he'd previously had no ability to do and filled him with hope for things that had never before seemed possible.

He'd woken up this morning to the memory of Annie in his arms. And he had known then that he wanted her in his life. He wanted a life with her. Here, in this place, the goodness of which he had finally let himself remember.

He didn't want to get on yet another airplane and fly to the other side of the world where he knew no one, had no ties.

Yet, how could he stay here now, loving Annie?

Fate had an awful sense of humor. The man who did not believe in life-changing love had just gotten his life changed by love. And the woman responsible for it wasn't available.

THAT AFTERNOON, Jack held a meeting in his father's old office with the two executives who had engineered the setup of the stolen goods. He showed them photos and a written statement from Early Gunter implicating them. He told them with steel in his voice that they were never to set foot on this property again, and if they did, he would take all the evidence he had to the county sheriff.

They left his office with their tails tucked between their legs, looking shell-shocked. Jack almost felt sorry for them. Almost.

He spent the rest of the afternoon holding meetings with key management, giving them an edited version of the cause of C.M.'s downward spiral, then laying out his strategy for turning the company around. Long term, he wasn't sure what he would do with the business, but for now, he only knew he wanted to give it back to the people who worked here.

As soon as the last of the stunned C.M. employees left the office, Jack picked up the phone and dialed Pete's cell phone.

"H'lo."

"You must be finished for the day. You sound entirely too cheerful."

"Matter of fact, I am. Big date tonight. When're you heading back to civilization?"

"Kind of wanted to talk to you about that. Think your car could make it this far past the city limits if you asked it nicely?"

Silence and then, "Play that again."

"We need to talk, Pete. Can you drive out here in the morning?"

"Sure, but why do I have a feeling I'm going to wish I hadn't?"

J.D. SLEPT IN the guest room.

The decision was not arrived at automatically.

He'd pulled out his bag of J.D. charm and tried several of his old tricks on her. "You look worn out, babe. How about a back rub?"

A long soak in her bathtub with the door locked worked just fine for Annie. Up to her neck in bubbles, she stared at the cordless phone at the corner of the tub.

Call him, Annie. Tell him you wouldn't take J.D. back if the offer came with a small private island.

But then how did she explain that she was trying to make J.D. come to his senses? Give him a visible reminder of the domesticity to which he was all but allergic.

It sounded ridiculous.

It was ridiculous.

But if it worked, it could prevent a legal battle involving Tommy. And if it didn't work, she would take J.D. to the mat in any courtroom he chose.

If she had any hope of being convincing, she needed to stay away from Jack.

And then there were the other roadblocks she'd

been putting under her microscope for consideration. Jack wasn't going to be here forever. He had a life in another place. How could what happened between them be anything more than temporary?

You don't think he took any of that seriously, do you, Annie? To a man like him, that was little more than entertainment for the boondocks.

He could never be happy here, a man who's used to traveling all over the world.

Maybe he could.

Stop! For now, she couldn't think about any of this. For now, she had to focus on wrestling her future with J.D. into a straitjacket.

The next morning, she got up with the sun. She left J.D. a note on the kitchen table, put Cyrus out in the backyard with an extra chew toy, then tugged a sleepy-eyed Tommy out the front door.

"Why do we have to leave so early, Mama?" he asked, rubbing one eye with the back of his fist.

"I have to help with the church bake sale, and we don't want to be late."

"Won't we be the first ones there?"

"Maybe, but it's good to be early."

Tommy looked skeptical but didn't argue. Annie made a detour through the Krispy Kreme drive-through and ordered a caffeine-laced bribe for Clarice. They weren't supposed to pick her up until eight, but Annie did not trust herself with a J.D. face-to-face this morning.

Tommy was quiet on the drive to Clarice's. "Everything all right?" Annie asked him.

Tommy shrugged. And then, a few seconds later, "Daddy says if you two can't work things out, he wants me to come live with him."

Annie's heart dropped. "And what do you think about that?" she asked, struggling to keep the panic from her voice.

Tommy looked down at his lap, silent for so long that Annie's chest felt as though it would explode. "I wish he would visit more often, but I wanna live with you, Mama."

Relief catapulted through her, leaving in its wake sorrow that her son should be put in this position. "Oh, baby, that's what I want, too," she said, squeezing his arm. "Can you just trust me that I'm going to make sure of that?"

He looked up at her and nodded. And Annie was grateful and relieved for the love in her son's eyes.

Krispy Kreme offerings in arm, she and Tommy landed on Clarice's front porch an hour ahead of schedule.

Clarice answered the door with hot curlers in her hair. "You're early?"

"Ah, you know how important it is to be early for the bake sale setup."

"It is?"

"It is."

Tommy shook his Krispy Kreme bag. "Mama, can I eat my doughnut now?"

"Sure can."

"Kitchen's all yours, Tommy," Clarice said.

Tommy bounded down the front hall. "We got you whole wheat, Aunt Clarice," he threw over his shoulder.

"You know better than to use my jokes!" she called after him.

Tommy giggled.

Clarice turned to Annie and whispered, "Couldn't stand another minute with J.D.?"

"He'd better break fast."

Clarice smiled and headed upstairs, tugging curlers from her hair as she went. "I guess we'll be early for the bake sale."

THEY COULD NOT have ordered a more perfect day.

The sky was a beautiful blue, not a single cloud marring its surface. The air held just enough of a nip to make a sweater comfortable.

The Lord's Acre Sale was one of the most anticipated events in Langor County. All the churches participated, regardless of denomination. Standing under the tent set up by Macon Point's First Baptist, Annie felt newly grateful to be a part of a community like this one. All around her, women from the congregation were busy pulling cakes and pies from Tupperware containers, setting them up on the tables at the edges of the tent.

Clarice had offered to operate the cash register since baking was not in her reportoire. Pitching was, though. She'd already sold more than a dozen cakes in add-on sales. And she was at it again. "Mrs. Teal, these cookies look wonderful, but did you see that apple walnut over at the corner of table one? Honest to goodness, I don't think I've ever seen a cake that moist. And it's so nice to stick in the freezer for unexpected company."

"What a good idea, dear. Well, maybe I'll just take a quick look."

"You go right ahead. I'll hold on to these cookies for you."

Watching, Annie smiled, grateful that she and Clarice had cleared the air between them.

Annie scanned the crowd as far out as she could see. Tommy to her right with a group of boys and girls playing Red Rover. J.D. coming through the front entrance.

No sign of Jack. He wasn't here. To her discredit, she'd been watching from the corner of her eye all morning. Disappointment hung inside her like a water-filled balloon.

She glanced at her watch and made her way over to the register where Clarice had just rung up another cake sale. "Dunking booth time."

Clarice shook her head, taking Mrs. Teal's money. "You're really going through with that?"

"Part of the mayor's job."

"I'd resign. Effective immediately."

Annie smiled. "It won't be that bad. I get to wear a wet suit."

"How about a shower cap?"

"And send all the men running? I don't think so."

Clarice laughed. "May your customers all have bad aim."

PETE ARRIVED IN Macon's Point just after eleven. He'd called Jack on the way, and they'd agreed to meet in the high school parking lot.

He pulled up in the old white Suburban he used for hunting trips, window rolled down. He was wearing a Redskins baseball cap and small-lens sunglasses. He'd given up smoking six months ago and taken up bubble gum, his jaw working it like a weightlifter building a bicep.

Leaning against the door of his car, Jack folded his arms across his chest and shook his head. "Afraid you were going to get ambushed on the way?"

Pete got out, chuckling. "West of D.C., it's travel at your own risk, isn't it?"

Jack clapped him on the shoulder. "I'll buy you lunch for the added risk factor."

"So what is this, anyway?"

"Lord's Acre Sale. County's been having them

every fall as far back as I can remember. Come on, you're in for a treat.''

They walked the perimeter of the parking lot, ending up outside the Second Presbyterian tent where they were selling chili faster than they could put it in bowls.

''Man, that's good,'' Pete said after they'd gotten theirs and headed back through the crowd.

''Let's see if we can find a spot on the sidelines,'' Jack said. They parked and ate.

''That hit the spot,'' Pete said when he'd emptied his bowl. ''So what's on your mind? The suspense is killing me.''

''Things have worked out a little differently with the factory than I anticipated. I'm thinking I'll stay on and run it a while.''

Pete's eyebrows shot toward the bill of his cap. ''Wow.''

''Any interest in buying me out of the consulting business?''

''Any interest in selling cheap?''

Jack laughed. ''No, but I'll entertain offers.''

''You're serious.''

Jack kicked a toe against the pavement and folded his arms across his chest. ''I can't do both, Pete. This feels like something I need to do. Like the outcome will matter to a lot of people.''

''Well, from a selfish standpoint, I wish like hell you didn't feel that way. But I understand why you would. I assume you think you can turn the business around, or you wouldn't be considering taking it on.''

''With a lot of hard work. I'm not kidding myself. It won't be easy. But I have to try.'' That was the feeling he couldn't shake. He had to try. This town had worked its way back into his heart, and he wanted to do what he could to make sure it didn't have to change. Staying here under the knowledge that he would likely run into Annie with J.D. felt like a club to the chest, but he was in too deep now to walk away.

To their right, a crowd began to gather around the dunking booth set up at the edge of the asphalt parking lot. Reverend Landers stepped forward and hung a sign on the front: DUNK THE MAYOR: $1

Annie appeared from the front, climbed the short ladder on the side, wearing a wet suit that defined her shape curve by curve. Jack's mouth went suddenly dry.

Pete pursed his lips in a silent whistle. ''Whoo. Is she available?''

''Get in line,'' Jack said.

Pete stuck his finger in his ear and waggled it around. ''Just when you think there aren't any surprises left. She wouldn't have anything to do with your sudden decision to turn country on me, would she?''

''You mean aside from the fact that she just got back with her ex-husband?''

Pete's face scrunched in disappointment. "Man. That sucks."

"Tell me."

They watched while a line formed straight out from the booth. Two boys took a shot with wind-up throws and missed. Three teenage girls, all giggling, followed without success. An older man took the next, and he missed. Another dozen takers lined up, all of whom missed. Good-natured laughter rumbled through the crowd.

Annie wiped her brow in comic relief.

Jack couldn't take his eyes off her. She was adorable. And he wanted her like he'd never wanted anything in his life.

"Honey, you can't sit in there and not get dunked even one time." This from J.D. who stepped out of the crowd up front near the booth.

"Hey, isn't that J.D.—"

"Yeah," Jack said before he could finish.

"That does suck."

"How about letting me take a shot?" J.D. pulled some money from his wallet and handed it to a surprised Reverend Landers.

The crowd went instantly silent.

Annie's face drained of color.

"Five shots," J.D. said. "All or nothing. If I miss, I'll pay double."

"Big of him, huh?" Pete said.

"Seems to be the kind of guy he is. All heart."

"You think he'll really dunk her?"

At that moment, J.D. took aim and threw.

Splash! Annie hit the water.

She stood up, smiling, looking, to her credit, as if J.D. were just any other citizen playing the game. She climbed back on the board, water streaming from her hair.

Not a man or woman in the crowd laughed. Or for that matter said a word.

The only person enjoying this seemed to be J.D. It was a little like watching someone spear fish in a bucket.

Pete leaned close to Jack. "Doesn't it say somewhere in the marriage manual that husbands aren't allowed to do that to wives?"

"They're not married anymore, but if it doesn't, it should." Jack raised a hand and called out, "You miss this one, how about giving me a shot with you in the booth?"

J.D. turned around, his gaze landing like a laser on Jack, as if he'd known exactly where he was standing. "Deal," he said, confidence oozing from the word.

He wound up, made an exaggerated pitcher's pose, threw. And missed.

The crowd erupted in a cheer. J.D.'s expression fell. He quickly put a smile back in place and said, "Deal's a deal."

Annie climbed out of the booth, took the towel

Reverend Landers handed her. Jack looked at her and winked.

Was it his imagination, or was there relief in her eyes?

"Five shots," Jack said, handing the Reverend his money.

J.D. pulled off his shoes—expensive-looking shoes—and climbed in. Jack wished he'd kept them on. He really wanted to get those shoes wet.

The area around the booth had gone completely quiet. The crowd had deepened, and people were standing on tiptoe to see.

Jack stepped up to the line, focused for a few seconds and threw the ball. He missed.

J.D.'s smile was practically blinding. "Don't choke now, Corbin," he said.

Jack picked up another ball, focused on the target, thought about the look on McCabe's face yesterday when he'd announced he and Annie were getting back together. He threw again.

This time, he didn't miss. J.D. hit the water with a satisfying ka-thwunk.

The crowd erupted in a roar of approval.

Jack did not look at Annie. He didn't dare.

J.D. climbed up, his expression decidedly more somber. "Everybody gets lucky once," he said.

Jack took aim and threw. Again, J.D. hit the water.

Another roar from the crowd. J.D. climbed back

up, looking a lot like the wet rat Jack personally thought him to be.

The fourth throw, Jack missed. J.D. got a little of his confidence back, crossed his arms across his chest and smiled.

"Last throw," Reverend Landers said. "Make it a good one, son."

Jack didn't disappoint. The last throw carried with it every ounce of his frustration that a guy like J. D. McCabe could end up with a woman like Annie.

The ball hit the target with a thump, and J.D. went down.

A simultaneous cheer went up from the crowd. "Whooo, Corbin! Way to go!"

For the first time since his return to Macon's Point, Jack felt as if he belonged. As if this were his team, and he mattered. He liked the feeling. He understood, then, what Annie had meant about belonging.

He let himself look at her then. Her gaze was pinned on him. She was smiling. He smiled back.

CHAPTER SEVENTEEN

STILL MANNING THE cash register for the bake sale, Clarice missed the excitement at the dunking booth. But she heard all about it from every customer who passed through the tent. Just the thought of seeing J.D. take a bottom-first dip into that booth made her want to go find Jack and hug his neck.

He was as good a guy as she'd pegged him to be from the start. And if she couldn't have him, she hoped Annie could.

"Last call at the First Baptist tent," she called out to passersby. "We've sold fifty-four cakes this morning. Only two left."

"I'll take them."

Clarice turned around to find a pair of amused brown eyes staring at her. Very nice, amused brown eyes. The rest of the package, at a quick glance, was pretty nice as well. He looked like someone who spent a good deal of time outdoors, red cheeks, a nose that had been sunburned a few times. "I have to charge extra if you buy both. They're all we have left."

The man let out a choked-sounding laugh. "You are good."

"I've heard that before."

"No doubt."

He was flirting with her. Clarice's face went warm. She was blushing! In a very uncharacteristic moment, she couldn't think of a thing to say.

"So what kind are they?"

"What?" she asked, distracted again by those brown eyes.

"The cakes."

"Oh, those. Ah, Myrtle, what were those two last cakes?"

The white-haired lady at the other end of the table scanned the tags on the boxes. "Carrot and white chocolate."

"Mmm," he said. "And if I bought them, could I talk you into a slice with some coffee or something?"

"Well, I...there's an offer I haven't had this morning. Appealing as it is, I don't make a habit of sharing cake with strangers."

"I have references," he said, palms raised.

"Really?"

"Really. That's my buddy over there." He turned and pointed. "He just defended the honor of the town mayor—"

"My sister."

"Your sister. Two lookers in the family."

Oh, all right, so flattery worked for her. "Jack's your buddy, huh?"

"He can tell you how harmless I am. When do you get off cake duty?"

"You just bought the last one. How about now?"

"Now sounds just right."

ANNIE CHANGED BACK into her clothes in the ladies' room of the high school gymnasium. She stood in front of the mirror drying her hair with the dryer she had thankfully brought with her. She couldn't get ready fast enough. Not another hour would pass where she let J.D. think they were getting back together. She had done nothing but insult herself for not standing up to him, for not telling him she would fight him tooth and nail for Tommy, and that he did not deserve either one of them.

No more games. She had put her heart into making a new life for Tommy and her. She liked her life. Wanted to keep it. J. D. McCabe was not going to take it away from her. Not a single piece of it.

Determination roared up from that place inside her where she had put away all the unaired slights accumulated during her marriage to J.D. It was time to pull them out again.

And just as soon as she'd done that, she intended to find Jack. She had some things to tell him, too.

A few minutes later, Annie hurried across the gymnasium parking lot. At the edge of the asphalt, J.D. was standing under an old maple tree talking to three members of the town council. His back was to her. She slowed several yards away from the group, and then stopped altogether.

J.D.'s voice carried clearly. "No doubt I couldn't

bat my eyelashes at Corbin with near the effectiveness my wife did. But is that the sole talent you expect from the mayor of this town? Eyelash batting?''

Uneasy laughter rippled out from the three men.

''Now, J.D., that might be a tad—'' Earnest Holt began.

Annie didn't wait to hear the response. She shot across the pavement with fury as a propellant. ''And you consider that my sole talent, J.D.?''

J.D. whirled around. ''Annie.''

All three council members looked as if they'd rather be anywhere else in the world at that moment.

''I know you may find this hard to believe, J.D. But there are some things in this world that people actually work for. Put their hearts into. Things that a new toy or a new dog just won't fix. The hard stuff has to be earned, J.D. You have to earn it.''

J.D.'s mouth twisted to one side. He started to speak, stopped, then with serious agitation said, ''Annie, can't this wait until we get home?''

''No, it can't. Because you don't have a home here. You gave that up. I have a home here. A place where I belong. Where I matter. It's one I intend to keep. And I'm not going to give any of it up just because you were hit with a temporary itch you needed to scratch. I'm staying here, J.D. Tommy is staying with me. And if it suits this council, I intend to finish out my term as mayor of this town. If you try to change any of that, I will give you a fight like nothing you've ever imagined. I will drag out every single rotten thing you ever did as a husband and father, J.D. And I will be ruthless.''

For once in his life, J.D. was speechless. He stood there, staring at Annie as if he had no idea who she was. As if she'd just dropped into the parking lot via a hole in the sky, species unidentifiable. He jerked and swung a glance at the three men standing behind him, all of whom were suddenly busy studying their shoes.

''You know what, Annie,'' J.D. poked a finger in her direction, his words stumbling out on a sputter. ''A woman like you does not deserve a man like me.''

''She most certainly does not.''

Jack stood a few feet to their right, his expression cold enough to instantly freeze boiling water.

Annie's heart fluttered, spun a circle like a top set in motion by something outside of its own ability to control.

J.D. slicked a hand across his hair, anchored it at the back of his neck, then blew out a whoosh of indignation. ''Do you people have any idea what my name alone can do for this town—''

''A name doesn't count for much without a person behind it who's willing to get in the trenches for the things they believe in.'' Jack again.

Annie set her gaze on him, and for the life of her could not pull it away.

''That's who Annie is, you know. Or maybe you never did know. And that, in my opinion, is an unimaginable shame. To think that a man could have a woman like her and not have any idea what he has.''

A wave of pure emotion hit Annie so hard she had to lock her knees to keep standing.

Jack looked at her then, really looked at her, his eyes clearly inviting her to see what he felt.

''If it weren't for Annie, Corbin Manufacturing would have already closed its doors. It took her love for this town and its people to make me see the effect that action would have had. How could Macon's Point have a better mayor than one who thinks its people are its greatest asset?''

J.D. puffed up as if he'd suddenly been injected with hot air. ''You know, Annie, this town has always been too small for me. But it's exactly right for you.'' He turned around and stomped off across the parking lot.

''I can't think of a nicer compliment,'' Annie said, turning to face Jack.

''Did I just overstep my bounds?'' he asked.

''A lady likes having her honor defended.''

Jack smiled. ''I like defending your honor. But you don't need me riding in on a white horse. You were doing just fine yourself.''

''This would be our cue to leave,'' Earnest said, waving for the other two council members to follow.

And suddenly, it was just the two of them, alone, or at least as alone as they could be with half the county on the other side of the parking lot.

Jack took her hand and pulled her around to the

other side of the maple tree. She stood with her back against the wide old trunk, unable to say a word, to do anything, in fact, other than pray that he would kiss her.

He kissed her.

Quickly, deeply, as if he, too, could think of little else.

Annie sighed and kissed him back, wrapped her arms around his neck and put heart and soul into it. "Jack," she said, her voice not sounding like her own.

He pulled back and looked down at her.

"Thank you. For everything you said."

"It was all true, Annie. When my dad married someone else so soon after my mom died, I looked at what he did as proof that he couldn't have loved her like I'd always thought. I think I was wrong about that. And wrong, too, that there would never be anyone who would make me feel that way."

Annie's eyes filled with tears. She reached up, touched a finger to his lips.

"It's like I had this sensor in my heart," he said, "and it never made a sound until I met you. You're the one. It's been telling me that from the first moment I saw you."

"Jack."

He put his arms around her waist, pulled her close to him and kissed her again. "Will you marry me, Annie?"

Not so very long ago, the question would have sent

her into a whirlwind of self-doubt. How could she know this was right? How could she be sure this time wouldn't be like the last time? That Jack was the man he seemed to be. The difference was that she knew it in the deepest part of her, in her heart. That this was the man with whom she wanted to spend the rest of her life. And that his feelings mirrored her own. She had to believe that this was how a person knew. "You know I come with a seven-year-old son, a very large St. Bernard and a sister who spends as much time at my house as she does her own?" Her voice broke a little at the end.

"Couldn't have designed a better package," he said, smiling and then gathering her against him for the kind of kiss that would have made any answer other than yes impossible.

EPILOGUE

Three Months Later

IF IT WERE possible for two people to die of waiting, both Jack and Annie would be long gone.

But the waiting was about to end, and Annie stood at the window of their hotel room, looking out at the full moon resting high over the water off St. John in the U.S. Virgin Islands. She looked down at the simple nightgown she'd chosen to wear, off-white with skinny straps and a scooped neckline. Clarice had helped her pick it out on a pre-honeymoon shopping spree to D.C. Annie hoped it wasn't too boring, hoped it appealed to Jack.

They'd gotten married that morning at the First Baptist Church in Macon's Point. A beautiful, snowy Saturday, it seemed as if most of the town had turned out for the wedding. Tommy served as ring bearer, Clarice as maid of honor and Pete as best man. Essie had sat on the front row with a tear-soaked tissue clutched in one hand.

J.D. had actually sent flowers and a respectful note saying he hoped Annie would allow Tommy to visit him in L.A. soon. He'd dropped the custody suit, and

surprised Annie the last few months with regular
phone calls to their son. Annie was glad. For
Tommy's sake, she wanted there to be peace between
them.

For Jack and her, these past three months had felt
like three years. But Annie had thought they needed
a stretch of time to make sure their feelings for one
another didn't change. To not let their very well-
proven physical attraction dictate their actions. And
she was now. Sure. Jack loved her. She had seen it
in his eyes numerous times these past few months,
quiet, anchored love, each glimpse of which deepened
her own acceptance of it.

Her husband loved her.

The bathroom door opened, light slicing the dark-
ened room in half. Annie turned around and looked
at him. Cliché that it was, he took her breath away.
His hair was damp from the shower. He wore dark
blue cotton pajama bottoms that hung low on his hips.
His chest was bare, and he was lean and muscled, fit.
There was something in the immediate intimacy of
the moment that made Annie mute with shyness.

Jack crossed the room, stopped just inches from
her, reached out and touched the back of his hand to
her face. "Hi, wife."

"Hi, husband."

"Sure do like the sound of that."

"I like it, too."

"Did you call home?"

Annie nodded. "Everything's fine. Clarice said

Tommy was already asleep. She and Pete were making popcorn."

"Kind of interesting that he postponed his trip back to London for a few days."

"Uh-huh. And Clarice happened to mention that she's always wanted to see Big Ben. I have a feeling she'll be going over for a visit."

"You all right with that?"

"Pete's great."

Jack put his arms around her, pulled her close. "You are so beautiful, Annie."

He leaned down and kissed her then, his hand slipping to the back of her neck, inviting her closer. Annie stepped in, wrapped her arms around his waist and opened her mouth to his in an invitation of her own.

They'd done a lot of kissing these past few months, on her front porch, under the maple tree in Sam and Ned's pasture, in Jack's office at C.M. Long, deep, taking-their-time kisses that were so decadently skillful that Annie never failed to sink against him with longing.

Now was no exception.

He dropped an arm to the back of her knees, picked her up and carried her over to the enormous bed in the center of the room.

He laid her down, gently, her head sinking onto soft pillows. Jack stood there for a moment, just looking at her, but Annie felt no shyness now. She believed in Jack's love for her, wanted to show him with heart and body.

She held a hand out. He took it, entwining his fingers with hers and stretching out alongside her.

The moon lent the room soft light, and they lay there in bed, smiling at one another, husband and wife. He ran the back of his hand across her cheek and hair and said, "I never knew what this could be like. Belonging to someone and having someone who belongs to me. It changes the way everything feels. Just the thought of making love to you, Annie, is…it's exactly that. Love."

He kissed her again then. Annie arched her back and settled her hands on his very nice shoulders. "Did anyone ever tell you you're awfully good at that?"

"I think you did once or twice," he said with a smile in his voice.

"I did, didn't I?"

"I kind of like hearing it, though."

"I probably won't get tired of saying it."

"I definitely won't get tired of kissing you."

"Promise?"

"Promise," he said, his leg slipping between hers, the closeness both longed-for and welcome.

The sound of the ocean dipped through the room's open windows, and the two of them watched each other while their bodies made their own greetings.

Annie ran her fingers through his hair, cupped her hand at the back of his neck. "If this was all there was, I'd be happy with it."

"Oh, but there's more," he said, smiling down at her, his hand finding the hem of her nightgown, then sliding from thigh to waist, his palm curving round her hipbone and the flat of her abdomen. "All right if I show you now?"

"I thought you'd never ask."

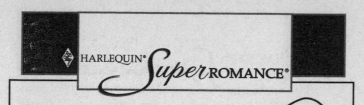

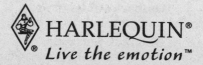

HARLEQUIN *Super*ROMANCE

Koomera Crossing

Welcome to Koomera Crossing,
a town hidden deep in the Australian Outback.
Let renowned romance novelist Margaret Way
take you there. Let her introduce you to
the people of Koomera Crossing.
Let her tell you their secrets....

Watch for

Home to Eden,
available from Harlequin Superromance
in February 2004.

And don't miss the other Koomera Crossing books:

Sarah's Baby
(Harlequin Superromance #1111, February 2003)

Runaway Wife
(Harlequin Romance, October 2003)

Outback Bridegroom
(Harlequin Romance, November 2003)

Outback Surrender
(Harlequin Romance, December 2003)

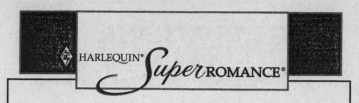

HARLEQUIN *Super*ROMANCE®

Crystal Creek **TEXAS**

If this is your first visit to the friendly ranching town located in the Texas Hill Country, get ready to meet some unforgettable people. If you've been here before, you'll recognize old friends... and make some new ones.

Home to Texas
by Bethany Campbell
(Harlequin Superromance #1181)
On sale January 2004

Tara Hastings and her young son have moved to Crystal Creek to get a fresh start. Tara is excited about renovating an old ranch, but she needs some help. She hires Grady McKinney, a man with wanderlust in his blood, and she gets more than she bargained for when he befriends her son and steals her heart.

Available wherever Harlequin Superromance books are sold.

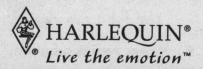

HARLEQUIN®
Live the emotion™

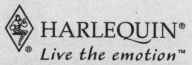

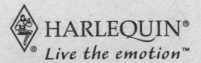